Then she saw the man who'd loosed the yell as he came into the fan of light spreading from the open doors. Her hand stopped suddenly, grasping the butt of her revolver, as he looked up at her and the light from the doorway showed his face.

What Jessie saw was an apparition from the past.

Though twin ivory-grip Colt revolvers were holstered at his hips on a gunbelt buckled on outside his frock coat, the new arrival made no move to draw. He stood for a moment gazing up at Jessie, then brought up his right hand very slowly and touched the brim of his hat. He held his arm raised, partly shielding his face and throwing it into shadow as he spoke.

"You ain't got a thing to worry about from me, ma'am," he said. "Wild Bill don't draw on ladies and children."

Also in the LONE STAR series
from Jove

LONGARM AND THE LONE STAR LEGEND

LONE STAR AND THE MOUNTAIN MAN

LONE STAR AND THE STOCKYARD SHOWDOWN

LONE STAR AND THE RIVERBOAT GAMBLERS

LONE STAR AND THE MESCALERO OUTLAWS

LONE STAR AND THE AMARILLO RIFLES

LONE STAR AND THE SCHOOL FOR OUTLAWS

LONE STAR ON THE TREASURE RIVER

LONE STAR AND THE MOON TRAIL FEUD

LONE STAR AND THE GOLDEN MESA

LONE STAR AND THE RIO GRANDE BANDITS

LONE STAR AND THE BUFFALO HUNTERS

LONE STAR AND THE BIGGEST GUN IN THE WEST

LONE STAR AND THE APACHE WARRIOR

LONE STAR AND THE GOLD MINE WAR

LONE STAR AND THE CALIFORNIA OIL WAR

LONE STAR AND THE ALASKAN GUNS

LONE STAR AND THE WHITE RIVER CURSE

LONE STAR AND THE TOMBSTONE GAMBLE

LONE STAR AND THE TIMBERLAND TERROR

LONE STAR IN THE CHEROKEE STRIP

LONE STAR AND THE OREGON RAIL SABOTAGE

LONE STAR AND THE MISSION WAR

LONE STAR AND THE GUNPOWDER CURE

LONE STAR AND THE LAND BARONS

LONE STAR AND THE GULF PIRATES

LONE STAR AND THE INDIAN REBELLION

LONE STAR AND THE NEVADA MUSTANGS

LONE STAR AND THE CON MAN'S RANSOM

LONE STAR AND THE STAGECOACH WAR

LONE STAR AND THE TWO GUN KID

LONE STAR AND THE SIERRA SWINDLERS

LONE STAR IN THE BIG HORN MOUNTAINS

LONE STAR AND THE DEATH TRAIN

LONE STAR AND THE RUSTLER'S AMBUSH

LONE STAR AND THE TONG'S REVENGE

LONE STAR AND THE OUTLAW POSSE

LONE STAR AND THE SKY WARRIORS

LONE STAR IN A RANGE WAR

LONE STAR AND THE PHANTOM GUNMEN

LONE STAR AND THE MONTANA LAND GRAB

LONE STAR AND THE JAMES GANG'S LOOT

LONE STAR AND THE MASTER OF DEATH

LONE STAR AND THE CHEYENNE TRACKDOWN

LONE STAR AND THE LOST GOLD MINE

LONE STAR AND THE COMANCHEROS

WESLEY ELLIS

LONE STAR

AND
HICKOK'S GHOST

JOVE BOOKS, NEW YORK

LONE STAR AND HICKOK'S GHOST

A Jove book/published by arrangement with
the author

PRINTING HISTORY
Jove edition/June 1988

ISBN: 0-515-09586-9

Chapter 1

"Yes, indeed, Miss Starbuck," the young desk clerk in the Livestock Yards Exchange Hotel told Jessie. "We received your telegram, and your usual accommodations are ready for you." He took a small ledger from a shelf below the registration desk and flipped through its pages. "Rooms 230 and 232. That would be a second floor corner bedroom for yourself and the room adjoining for Mr. Ki."

"Then we'll go right up," Jessie said, as she finished signing the register and pushed the heavy book across the desk to the clerk. "But first, tell me if you have a gentleman named Lucas Perry staying here. He hasn't moved his office into the Exchange Building yet, and when we stopped by his office in the yards we found it closed."

"Perry?" The clerk repeated the name thoughtfully, then shook his head. "I'm afraid not. The name's familiar, though. Just a moment, let me look at the ledger."

As the clerk disappeared around the partition that

1

shielded the hotel's office from the lobby, Ki said, "If Perry's been in Fort Worth for a while he's probably moved into a house or a flat somewhere close to the stockyards. We shouldn't have any trouble finding him, even if his office is closed."

"Oh, we're not in that big a hurry," Jessie told him. "In fact, a little bit of a delay might be a help to us, Ki. It's too late for his office to be open today, and if we don't get to see him until tomorrow we'll have time to ask a few of the other brokers what they think about him, and what sort of man he is."

Before Ki could reply the clerk returned. "Mr. Perry kept a room here for several weeks after he arrived from Chicago, Miss Starbuck, but he left more than a month ago. I have his address for you, though." Handing Jessie a slip of paper, he went on, "He moved into one of the flats in a new building on Twelfth Street; here's the number of the building."

"Thank you," Jessie said. "We'll find him without any trouble, I'm sure." She turned back to Ki and said, "Let's go to his flat now, Ki. Whether we find him or not, we can come back here and rest a bit before we have dinner. It's still early, and we can decide later what—" Jessie stopped short as a new voice broke in on her remark to Ki.

"Jessie Starbuck!" a man behind them exclaimed. "I wasn't sure at first that it was you, not until I got close."

Turning toward the man who'd spoken, Jessie smiled when she saw his face. "Courtney Mays!" she said. "What a pleasant surprise!"

"I might say the same thing," the young man told her. He nodded to Ki, and as Ki replied with a half-bow, he went on, "What's brought you here from the Circle Star, Jessie? Surely you've shipped out your market herd before now?"

2

"Several weeks ago, Court," Jessie replied. "But I suppose you could say that's why Ki and I are here."

Mays frowned. "I'm afraid I don't follow you."

"It's much too long a story to tell now," Jessie answered. "But I'd like to visit with you about the problem that's brought us here, if we can find a bit of time. Ki and I just got in, and I'm anxious to take care of one little matter before I plan to do anything else."

"I've got some trail dust to get rid of myself," Mays told her. "I just rode in from the Bar M. Suppose we have dinner together, Jessie? And of course you'll join us, Ki."

"Thank you, Mr. Mays," Ki said. "But I have a number of Oriental friends in Fort Worth, and I always visit them when we come here. I'm sure you and Jessie will find enough to talk about, dining together."

"Of course." Mays nodded. "It's been quite a while since we've seen each other." After glancing at the big clock on the wall above the registration desk, he turned back to Jessie. "It's almost four o'clock now. A late dinner, then? Seven o'clock, in the dining room?"

"That'll be fine," she answered. "I've run into something that gives me an idea that all of us ranchers just might have a problem. We'll compare notes and see if my suspicion is right."

In the hackney cab going to the address given them by the clerk at the hotel, Jessie said, "You know, it's just occurred to me that we might be rushing things a bit, Ki."

"Being in such a hurry to see Perry?"

Jessie nodded. "I want our visit to be a total surprise to him. If I hadn't wanted to take him off-guard, I'd have sent him a telegram to expect us when the train stopped in San Antonio."

"He'll be just as surprised when you knock on the door

3

of his flat as he'd be if you walked into his office when he wasn't looking for you," Ki pointed out.

"I suppose you're right," Jessie said, and nodded again. "We'll go ahead, then, since we're already in the cab."

"His office in the stockyards being closed this early in the day is a perfect excuse for you to try to catch him at home," Ki went on. "But if you want to avoid seeing him until later, I can go to the door of his flat while you wait in the cab. I'll just tell him you'll be calling on him at his office tomorrow and wanted to be sure he'd be there. He needn't even know we came to his flat together."

"That might be a shrewd idea," Jessie agreed. "Suppose we handle it that way."

Lucas Perry's address proved to be an imposing three-story brown brick structure with a wide entry-way up a half-flight of limestone steps. The windows were framed in terracotta casings, and the building stood apart from the few other buildings on the street, which had obviously been opened for development quite recently. Jessie sat back in the cab while Ki went to the door. He was inside for only a few moments.

"Perry wasn't at home either," he reported. "So I left a message with his landlord. I told him to look for you to call at his office sometime tomorrow morning."

"Good," Jessie returned. "I'm just as glad we missed him. If he has any reason to be worried about me coming to see him, he'll have it on his mind overnight. That ought to make him just a bit nervous at the prospect of seeing me. And I'll still have time to rest a bit from that train trip before I sit down to dinner with Courtney Mays."

"Let's enjoy just one glass of champagne before we start swapping stories about our problems, Jessie," Courtney Mays suggested.

He was working the cork out of the towel-swathed champagne bottle as he spoke. It yielded with a healthy pop, and a breath of white mist floated from the bottle's neck. Courtney filled Jessie's glass, then his. The light amber wine under its surface coating of tiny frothy bubbles looked very good to Jessie. She nodded, raised her glass and touched it to his. They sipped the wine slowly, silent for a moment.

"This is really enjoyable after that long, hot train ride from the Circle Star," Jessie said. "I'm sure your horseback ride from the Bar M was a lot more pleasant than my trip on the train. You had a cool breeze on your face, while I had to keep fighting cinders."

"I had a breeze on the way here, but at this time of year it's not very cool anywhere south of the Red River—or north of it until you get somewhere up in Canada, for that matter. But what you said in the lobby has had my curiosity working overtime. Suppose you tell me why you came all the way from the Circle Star to Fort Worth, Jessie."

"A pretty well-founded suspicion that this new cattle broker who's taken over Emerson White's business is doing some cheating at my expense."

"But you're not sure yet?"

"No. As long as Emerson was handling our cattle sales, I never had to worry. He and Alex were old friends, and Emerson became—well, I guess it'd be like he was an unofficial uncle to me. I trusted him, just as Alex did."

"Yes, Emerson was one of the old-timers here at the Fort Worth stockyards," Mays said, nodding. "He handled all of Dad's sales for years, and I—well, I just took the attitude that I'd inherited him from Dad, along with the ranch."

"I'm afraid the firm that bought his business when he died doesn't operate the way Emerson did," Jessie went

5

on. "Have you been facing the same problem I have?"

"I haven't had any arguments with the new man, if that's what you mean." Mays frowned, refilling Jessie's glass. "Of course, I haven't met him face to face yet, so there'd be no reason for us to get crossways."

"I haven't met him, either. Not yet, at least."

"Then what's your problem with him?"

"Too many steers reported dying on the way from the Circle Star to the stockyards here," Jessie replied. "I have a hunch this new broker's cutting out a few head from our shipments and selling them on his own account."

"That used to be a pretty common trick in the old days," Mays said thoughtfully. "But there weren't very many brokers then, either."

"Or any stockyards south of Chicago," Jessie added. "When Alex was first putting the Circle Star together, he sold his market herds to a wholesale butcher in San Antonio."

"So did my father, Jessie," Mays said. "Except that the butcher was in Kansas City. But the railroads changed all that, Jessie. And I know that steers do die when they're crowded into cattle-cars for a long time, and the animals in your shipments from the Circle Star stay on the train a lot longer than—well, than mine would, shipping from the Bar M. That might have something to do with it."

Jessie shook her head. "I've been going over our records, Court. We've always lost a few head out of our shipments, but during all the years that Emerson White was in business he never reported more than twenty or thirty dead animals in the shipment when it got here to Fort Worth. This new man, Perry, reported that there were more than seventy-five steers taken out of the cattle-cars last year and a hundred and fifteen this year."

"That's a sizable jump, all right. More than double."

"Yes. And for no real reason that I can see," Jessie went on. "I've asked the stationmaster at our little whistle-stop about that. I know they're not overcrowding the cattle-cars, because I watch them being loaded, even if it means staying at the station for almost a week."

"It's a slow process." Mays nodded. "With a herd the size of mine, and getting about thirty head into each car, it takes two days for us to load out a train at the Bar M."

"But I can't find any reason why the number of dead cattle has been increasing at such a rate in the Circle Star herds," Jessie went on. "I've asked the station agent, but all he can say is what I've seen myself. Oh, he's found out a few things for me. I know that the trains are routed the same distance, they make the same number of watering stops at the same places—nothing's changed, except that we keep losing a few more head from each shipment."

"What you're really saying, then, is that you suspect the new livestock brokerage outfit that took over Emerson White's business after he died is sending you falsified reports."

"That's the only possible conclusion," Jessie said.

"One thing I like about driving cattle to market is being able to see that the herd gets the right attention," Mays said thoughtfully. "I'll have to admit we could ship by train a lot more efficiently. It'd very likely cost less, but as long as I can, we'll drive."

"Well, the losses from cattle deaths aren't going to make or break the Circle Star," Jessie went on. "But it's been my experience that crookedness in one part of a business usually means that there's some in another part as well."

"You're talking now about falsifying other records as well as the shipment deaths?" Mays frowned.

"What would stop a broker from shaving a few dollars here and there off his sales-receipts figures?" Jessie asked.

7

Mays was silent for a moment. Then he nodded slowly and said, "Nothing that I can see. I'm sure we get the same kind of sales reports at the Bar M that you do at the Circle Star, and they're just copies made in the broker's office from the tallies he's given by the Exchange."

"That's exactly the point," Jessie agreed. "We're blind on all sides, Court. If a broker sends us false reports, the only way we can find out we're being robbed is to go to the Exchange office and compare their records with ours."

"And that's what you've come here to do?"

"Yes, of course. I'd still be enjoying the peace and quiet of the Circle Star if I hadn't noticed the unusually high number of cattle deaths."

"A hundred and fifteen, you said a minute ago. Out of how many head, Jessie?"

"Since we began sending our cattle on the railroad to Fort Worth instead of driving our market herd to San Antonio, we've been shipping about thirty thousand head after every roundup."

"I've been curious since we ran into each other, Jessie," Mays went on. "Just what do you plan to do about this fellow who took over from Emerson White?"

Jessie took another sip of champagne before replying. Then she said, "If he's been stealing from me by falsifying the number of cattle deaths in the Circle Star herd, I'll have enough evidence to file embezzlement charges against him. I don't have much sympathy for thieves."

"Neither do I. But I meant about finding another broker. If this Lucas Perry's stealing cattle from you, the chances are he's robbing me, too. Maybe not the same way, but by sending me forged bills of sale, or some other scheme."

"Why, I'll change to another broker, of course."

Mays nodded. "That's what I plan to do, too."

"It may take a little time to find somebody we can

trust," Jessie went on. "But we'll both be better off."

"With herds as big as the ones you're shipping, you won't have to do any looking," Mays told her. "There'll be brokers forming a line a mile long in front of your door as soon as the word gets around that you're changing."

"That's what I don't want to see happen," Jessie said. The serious set of her face told Mays that she was not making a joke. She went on, "I don't want Perry to hear that I suspect him until I can be sure he's stealing from me."

"How do you propose to go about doing that?"

"I'll talk to him first." Jessie frowned thoughtfully as she spoke. "I want to hear his side of the story. If his explanation doesn't satisfy me, I'll press him for details."

"Suppose you're still not satisfied?"

"Then I'll ask to see the actual tally sheets that were made out by the foreman of the stockyards crew that unloaded our Circle Star cattle. If I find anything that looks suspicious in them, or if Perry refuses to show them to me, I'll go to Arthur Pierce and look at the records the men hired by the yards gave him when they unloaded our cattle-cars."

"I can only see one hole in your plan, Jessie."

"And what is it?"

"Unlikely as it is, suppose Pierce is working in cahoots with Perry?"

Jessie shook her head. "He wouldn't be. Arthur would never do anything crooked, anything that would harm the stockyards. He's the one who had the idea of turning Fort Worth into the big-time cattle-shipping center that it's gotten to be."

"Yes, I'm sure you're right about that." Mays nodded. "I think I'd trust Arthur with anything I've got. But even though it's unlikely, stranger things have happened."

9

"I'll take my chances that my plan will work," Jessie said. Her voice reflected the confidence she felt after their long discussion. If there'd been any flaws in the course of action she'd proposed, she was sure that Courtney Mays would have seen them. She looked at her companion now. Mays had lifted the champagne bottle out of the ice-bucket and was hefting it, trying to determine how much wine it still held.

"I think I'd better order another bottle," he said. "There's only a little bit left here, and since we've started on champagne, we might as well drink it with our dinner."

"You've just reminded me how hungry I'm getting." Jessie smiled. "Shouldn't we start eating about now?"

"If you're ready, so am I." Turning in his chair, he caught the eye of their waiter. When the man came to the table, he said, "Another bottle, and we're ready to start supper when you bring it."

"Goodness!" Jessie exclaimed. "That was a wonderful dinner, Court. Between it and the champagne, I feel relaxed and at peace with the world."

"In spite of the job that's waiting for you tomorrow?"

"In spite of anything. If I was back at the Circle Star right now, I'd feel like saddling Sun and taking a ride across the prairie in the moonlight."

"That's a nice idea, but after spending two days in the saddle getting here from the ranch, I'm more inclined to think about it being bedtime."

"Yes, it is getting late," Jessie agreed. "And I'm sure you've got a full day ahead of you tomorrow, just as I have."

"Full day or no full day, Jessie, you're such charming company that I hate to see it coming to an end."

"I've enjoyed our evening, too."

After a moment's hesitation, the young rancher said, "It doesn't have to end right now, you know. I'm not very good at sweet talk, but if you get as lonesome on the Circle Star as I do on the Bar M, we've got more in common than we've ever talked about."

Jessie looked searchingly at her companion. He was looking at her with a look she had no trouble translating into the words which he seemed unable to find. It was not in Jessie's makeup to dissemble, to pretend that she did not understand his unuttered suggestion.

"Talking doesn't have a great deal to do with what you're suggesting, does it?" she asked, smiling.

"Very little, I suppose. And I've seen enough of you to know that you're not the kind of shy, retiring woman who pretends not to understand what I'm so clumsy about trying to say. I guess I'd just better come out with it flat-footed. Will you come to my room with me, Jessie?"

"I won't pretend, either. What are we waiting for, Court?"

Chapter 2

Waking as the cool dawn breeze billowed the lace curtains at the window, Jessie sat up, then propped herself up in the bed, leaning on her elbow. She looked down in the dim light at Courtney Mays, and a smile of pleasant memories grew on her face as she studied the muscular form and rugged features of the young rancher. Mays was still asleep, and Jessie resisted the temptation to touch him and waken him at once.

She felt pleasantly relaxed, now that she'd ended the long period of self-imposed continence she'd spent at the Circle Star; but with the new day showing on the horizon as a sliver of white pre-sunrise dawn she realized that her hours of freedom must end soon. Jessie laid her hand softly on Court's matted chest. He did not stir. Leaning forward, she continued her gentle caress, carrying her palm lightly down his chest to his muscle-corded stomach and waist.

When his deep regular breathing continued uninterrupted by her soft touch, Jessie moved her palm farther down, stroking the sleeping man's skin as lightly as a feather. She brushed her fingers as gently as possible through the bridge of his coarse pubic curls and placed the tips of her fingers on Court's quiescent cylinder. It was lax and yielding to her careful touch. She was beginning to become aroused by now, recalling again the fierce thrusts of that same fleshly appendage during their night together.

Stirred by her memory, Jessie bent over her still-sleeping lover and began caressing him with her lips and tongue. Court mumbled incoherently and stirred a bit, but his deep sleep remained unbroken. Even though he was still lost in the depths of slumber, he was responding to Jessie's carefully soft lips and her agile tongue. He began swelling, and soon was fully erect, still without having his sleep broken.

Jessie continued her attentions, using the tongue-caresses taught her by the wise old geisha to whom Alex had entrusted her sexual education. She was beginning to feel aroused herself when Court suddenly woke with a startled gasp.

"You've got a wonderful way of waking a man up," he said as he propped himself up on an elbow and looked down at her. "But won't you enjoy it more if we share?"

Jessie needed no further suggestion. She rose and straddled her lover, then dropped her hips heavily to impale herself on his swollen shaft. They lay quietly for a few moments, rocking in gentle unison as they recaptured the thrills they'd shared before sleep took them. They said nothing, but as their sensations mounted Court grasped Jessie's hips and held her to him while he reversed their position and began driving.

Jessie was more than ready to respond, and Court had almost reached his brink. He plunged into her fiercely

14

while her body writhed as her passion increased and they entered the final moments of their mutual frenzy. Then they peaked, almost in unison, uttering small cries of delight, shaking and gasping until the moments passed and they lay lax and motionless, Court's weight resting heavily on Jessie's pliant body.

After a while Court said, "I thought last night was good, but this morning's better."

He started to thrust again, slowly and gently because of his flaccid condition, but Jessie put her hands on his chest and gently pushed him upward. "This place is going to be busy in just a little while," she reminded him. "And I've got to go the full length of the hall to get to my room. I'd just as soon do that before the hall's full of men getting ready to go down to breakfast, and servants hurrying back and forth."

"You've got a point," he agreed. "But maybe later today? Or again tonight?"

"Are you going to be here that long?"

"Well, I didn't plan to be. Matter of fact, I aimed to go on back to the ranch as soon as I wound up my business today. But I sure don't want to leave while you're still here."

"We'll have to wait and see what happens today," she replied. She scrambled out of bed and began dressing. "If I can stay here another day, you know that I will."

"I'll count on you doing that, then. Will you leave a note for me at the desk when you're sure of your plans?"

"Of course."

Jessie was fully dressed by now. She stepped up to the bed and bent down to give her lover a good-bye kiss, then hurried down the hall to her own room. Pouring water from the pitcher on the nightstand into the washbowl, she sponged quickly and was dressed and ready when a light tapping at her door told her that Ki was also awake and around. She opened the door for him. If he noticed that her bed had not been disturbed, he made no comment.

"Is it too early for us to go to the stockyards?" he asked.

"It won't be by the time we've had breakfast," she replied. "And I'm as hungry as a mother lobo."

They had an unhurried breakfast in the dining room, and then started winding through the maze of holding-pens toward the old business section of the yards, where the office that had belonged to Emerson White was located.

As always on the rare occasions when Jessie had visited the stockyards, Jessie saw that the place was aboil with activity. The small square pens that stretched over almost a hundred acres turned the treeless prairie into a giant checkerboard. In the passageway that divided the pens into sections the yard's cowboys were riding from one pen to another, bunching cattle for shipment. Most of the pens Jessie and Ki passed were full of market-bound steers, and the smell of fresh manure filled the air along with the blatting complaints of the animals that were now confined in pens after having spent their short lives being free to graze on the open range.

Though the alleys between the pens were wide, many of them were clogged with small bunches of steers being moved from the pens to be loaded for shipment into the stock-cars that stood waiting on one or another of the railroad spurs that lanced across the yards at intervals. Between the noises made by the cattle and the shouts of the hands bunching and cutting them, Jessie and Ki found conversation difficult.

At last they reached the building which had housed Emerson White's brokerage office for as long as Jessie could remember. The door of the small structure was ajar, White's name in gold-leaf lettering still on the glass panel set into the weathered door. Jessie led the way inside without knocking. A man in his thirties sat at a rolltop desk, his back to the door. The desk, a pair of tall oak filing cabinets, and a rectangular table pushed against the wall opposite the desk were the room's only furnishings. When the man sitting at the desk heard Jessie's and Ki's footsteps on the bare splintered floor he turned in his high-backed swivel chair.

"Are you looking for somebody?" he asked.

"Yes," Jessie nodded. "For Mr. Lucas Perry."

"Well, you've found him. I'm Perry," the man at the desk replied.

Jessie was studying Perry as he spoke. During the busy, active years she'd passed through since Alex Starbuck's untimely death she'd learned through necessity to size up a man's character quickly.

Even though Perry was seated, she could tell that he was a stocky man, with pudginess just a few years in his future. His voice came from thin lips and grated like sandpaper on a rough board, while his thick sand-colored eyebrows drew together questioningly. Under their bristles he peered at her with small light-blue eyes as he said, "If you're looking for work, you'd better hyper back to the Livestock Exchange Building and ask there. I'm not hiring any office help, or help of any kind, right now."

"That's not exactly what we've come here for," Jessie told him. "My name is Jessica Starbuck. I own the Circle Star Ranch, and though you've acted as my cattle broker since Mr. White's death, this is the first time I've had the opportunity to come to Fort Worth and meet you. The gentleman with me is Ki, my assistant. We have a few matters to discuss with you, Mr. Perry."

While Jessie talked, Perry's offhand attitude had changed. He was looking from Jessie to Ki with real interest now. "Starbuck, sure," he said nodding. "The Circle Star ranch, way down in the southwest part of the state. Well, I won't let on that I'm not surprised. You're quite a ways from home, Miss Starbuck."

"I thought the best thing to do was come here and talk with you in person, Mr. Lucas," Jessie told him. "Letters aren't always the most satisfactory way of solving a problem."

"You're sorta taking me by surprise." Perry frowned. "I didn't know you and me had any problems, Miss Starbuck."

"Perhaps the problem isn't between us," Jessie went on. "It may be the fault of the railroad. That's one of the things I need to find out."

"Well, go ahead," Perry invited.

He did not invite them to sit down, but while he and Jessie talked Ki had pulled the chairs from the table up to Perry's desk. Jessie sat down and Ki followed suit.

"I'm concerned about the number of steers you reported dying in our last shipment while it was on the way here, Mr. Perry," she began. "I'm sure you know how much money we ranchers lose when cattle die in the cars in such large number."

"What gives you an idea like that?" Perry countered. "I don't charge you any commission on dead steers, Miss Starbuck; you're bound to know I don't. Any way you want to look at it, I'm outta pocket just the same as you are."

"Not quite the same," Jessie replied coolly. "You only lose your commission on their sale. That's just a small fraction of what the rancher who's raised the steer loses."

"Miss Starbuck, you know I'm not responsible for your steers until they're in the pens here in the yard," Perry said. "If you got a complaint, you better go see the I and

18

GN freightmaster. The railroad loaded your herd into the cattle-cars, and their men was supposed to look after the critters on the way here—give 'em water and feed and all like that."

"Oh, I intend to talk to the railroad, too," Jessie assured the broker. "In fact, when Ki and I leave your office, we'll be going to see the manager of the I and GN shipping office here at the stockyards."

"You ought to've gone there instead of coming to me," Perry told her, his voice sour. "I've got more important things to do than sit around and chatter about something that I'm not even responsible for in the first place."

"I've never even hinted that I considered you responsible for any cattle losses, Mr. Perry." Jessie's voice was level but not conciliatory. She went on, "However, I do need to be sure that I have very accurate figures when I go to the railroad office to complain. I want to compare the loss figures you sent me with the original report that the railroad people gave you."

Perry did not reply for a moment. Then he said, "All I can give you is a copy of the report I sent you, Miss Starbuck, and I'm sure you brought that along with you."

"Of course." Jessie nodded. "What I want now is a copy of the report the railroad gave you."

"Why, I've already sent that to our main office," Perry replied. "That's what they require me to do."

"And you didn't keep a copy in your files here?" Jessie tried to keep her disbelief from showing in her voice.

"Sure. That's what I just said, the copy in my files is the same as the one I suppose you've brought along. You'd be wasting your time going to the I and GN office, anyhow."

"Why do you say that?" Jessie frowned. "From the time my steers are loaded into I and GN stockcars at the Circle

Star spur until they're unloaded here at the stockyards, the railroad is responsible for them."

"Don't you think I know that?" Perry retorted. "But if I kept all the copies of all the papers I have to send customers like you, and all the papers you and my other customers send me, and all the forms and bills of lading and stuff that I get from the railroad and from other brokers, I'd need a two-story building to hold them, and two or three clerks just to make copies of them and keep them in order."

"Then you send all the original forms to your main office?" Jessie asked. Then she added, "That's in Chicago, I believe?"

"Yep. They've got a lot more room than I have to stack papers in, and plenty of clerks to keep track of them."

Ki had been sitting in patient silence while Jessie and Perry carried on their conversation. Now he said, "Perhaps I have a suggestion that would be helpful, Jessie."

"Go ahead." She nodded

"When we go to the railroad office, all that we'll need is the exact number of dead steers the men found in the cars when they were unloaded here in Fort Worth." Ki went on. "That should not be hard to get. If Mr. Perry doesn't have the information here, he can simply send a telegram to his main office and ask them to wire him the figures we need. We should have a reply in just a few hours."

"Of course!" Jessie agreed. She turned back to Perry. "I think Ki's come up with the right answer. Surely you can get the information we need by sending a wire to Chicago and asking them to wire it to you as soon as possible."

"Yeah, I guess I can do that," the broker replied. "It'll take a little while, three or four hours, I'd guess, to give them time to dig out the reports I sent 'em."

"Suppose we come back right after lunch, then," Jessie suggested. Turning to Ki, she went on, "That will give us

20

time to go to the Circle Star on the evening train if we can get our business here finished during the afternoon, since Mr. Perry is being so obliging."

"Glad I can help you, Miss Starbuck," Perry said. "I've found out already that your ranch was one of Mr. White's best customers, and I hope you'll just keep on giving me your business, now that he's gone."

Even when he was trying to be polite, Jessie found his manner and rough voice irritating. She nodded and told him, "At the moment, I don't have any plans to change."

"I'm glad to hear that," Perry replied. "Now, I better get moving myself if I'm going to have your figures in time."

"We'll be back about one o'clock, then," Jessie said. An afterthought occurred to her as she spoke, and she went on, "Unless you're having lunch at the restaurant in the stock-yards hotel. If you are, you can just leave the information I'm after at the hotel desk."

"That's what I'll do, then, if I get the wire from my head office before noon," Perry agreed. "It might take them a little while to dig out the figures, though."

As Jessie and Ki started back to the hotel, Ki said with a thoughtful frown, "Didn't Perry strike you as being a little bit nervous when you introduced yourself?"

"Both nervous and irritated," Jessie agreed. "He didn't really seem very cordial until we were leaving."

"He acted like he was glad to be rid of us."

"That's about what I thought, too. I can't say that he impressed me very favorably, Ki. When we get back to the hotel, I'm going to stop in at the stockyards office and talk to Arthur Pierce about him."

In the Livestock Exchange office, which occupied a good part of the combined hotel and office building, the manager of the Exchange came out to greet Jessie when his clerk took her name in to him.

21

"Jessie Starbuck!" he exclaimed. "You don't honor us with a visit very often. I'm glad you finally remembered us."

"Oh, you're not forgotten." Jessie smiled as they shook hands. "And I'm sure you remember Ki."

"Of course. He was always with your father when he stopped here." After Ki and Pierce shook hands, the Exchange man turned back to Jessie and asked, "Is this just a friendly call, or is there something I can help you with?"

"I'm looking for information," Jessie replied.

"I hope it's not about cattle prices," Pierce said. "Right now they seem to be going down. But I suppose you know that."

"They'll go up after all the summer range-herds have been shipped to market," Jessie said. "But cattle prices aren't my chief concern now. I'm looking for information."

"I'll be glad to help you if I can. What is it you want to know?"

For a moment Jessie hesitated. Then she suggested, "Maybe we'd better go into your office, where we can talk privately."

"I gather that this information you want is something of a confidential nature?"

Jessie nodded. "I suppose you'd call it that."

"Then I appreciate your suggestion, Jessie. I don't like to have confidential conversations out here where anyone who's passing by might overhear."

Settled into easy chairs in the stockyards manager's office, Jessie began, "Of course you know that when Emerson White died his business was bought by some brokerage firm in Chicago. I'm a bit curious about them. I'm sure you investigated them before you allowed them to operate here on the stockyards."

"We certainly did!" Pierce replied. "And their reputation

22

is very good. After I got my reports on them, I didn't hesitate to transfer Emerson's office to them."

"And the man they sent here to run the office?" Jessie asked. "Did you investigate him, too?"

Pierce shook his head. "No. As long as the people who pay Lucas Perry's wages are satisfied, we are, too. Unless he does something outrageous—swindling the ranchers who bring their cattle here, something of that sort. If that happened, we'd hold both him and his firm to account. I hope you're not having trouble with Perry."

"I'm not sure whether I am or not." Jessie frowned. "But I hope to have an answer before the day's out."

"Could you give me a hint?" Pierce asked.

"Let me ask you a question before I answer that," Jessie countered. When Pierce nodded she went on. "Did you have any reports of unusually large numbers of steers dying in stock-cars this past shipping season?"

"Nothing unusual," he replied. "I'm sure the brokers who operate in the yards would've mentioned a thing like that, but all I recall hearing about was a dozen head here, a half-dozen there. Really nothing to worry about."

"Would you call almost a hundred and twenty dead steers in our last shipment from here unusual?" she asked.

A frown growing on his face as he spoke, Pierce replied, "I certainly would!"

"And more than fifty head were reported dead in the cars when they got to Chicago last year," Ki put in.

"But last year we had practically no shipping deaths!" Pierce protested. "Two or three in a few cars, never more than eight or ten!"

"What Ki and I have given you are the figures reported by the company that took over Emerson's business," Jessie said quietly.

"You're talking about something like two hundred dead

steers," Pierce mused aloud. "That's a lot of money to any-body, Jessie."

"I've already done my arithmetic," Jessie told him. "It comes to almost sixty thousand dollars. Of course, losing the money's not going to break the Circle Star, but when someone steals from me, I get angry."

"And both these shipments were made after Emerson White's death, when this firm in Chicago had taken over his accounts," Pierce said thoughtfully. "I think this calls for an Exchange investigation, Jessie."

"No, Arthur," Jessie replied quickly. "Ki and I are here to make our own investigation. If other cattle ranches are involved, we'll find that out, too. But right now, I want to keep what's happening strictly confidential."

"I'll guarantee that it will be, Jessie," Pierce promised. "Now, it's going to take me several hours to get replies to the telegrams I'll have to send. If you and Ki will come back at—oh, say three o'clock, I'll have a lot more information to give you."

"We'll be here," Jessie replied. "And in the meantime, we just might do a little investigating of our own."

Chapter 3

"What sort of investigating did you have in mind, Jessie?" Ki asked as they walked through the wide, blue and white tile-floored corridor that connected the stockyards office and the hotel.

"There aren't too many livestock brokers who have offices here in the yards," Jessie replied. "But we might find out something helpful by asking them a few questions. I can't think of anyone except perhaps Arthur Pierce who'd know more about what a broker is doing than one of his competitors would."

"You're right, competitors do keep an eye on one another," Ki said. "And since Pierce will be waiting in his office for an answer to the wire he's sending to Chicago, we might uncover something about Perry right here in the yards."

"And we might also ask about steers dying during shipment this year," Jessie went on thoughtfully. "There might

25

be some new kind of cattle sickness spreading, and as isolated as we are down on the Circle Star, we might not have heard anything about it. If there is, we ought to find out."

"Two birds with one stone," Ki agreed.

"Then after we've visited with Court for a few minutes, let's walk back along the runways and talk to the nearest brokers," Jessie said.

They did not see Court Mays in the hotel lobby, and knocking on the door of his room brought no response. Jessie said, "We have more than an hour before lunch, Ki, and there are two brokers' offices just a few steps away from here. Let's go start asking questions now."

At the first office they visited, a small one-room affair very much like the one occupied by Perry, the broker nodded as soon as Jessie introduced herself.

"I've heard Em White mention you and your daddy a lot of times, Miss Starbuck," he said. "And Em was a real old friend of mine. I miss him, but I guess we've all got to go sometime. Why, we was the first livestock brokers to open up shop here in the yards. Had some real tight times together, me and Em did, but we always managed to pull out of 'em."

"I hope you're getting along as well with Emerson's successor, Mr. Gordon," Jessie replied. "I met him for the first time this morning."

"Well, he don't mix much with us old-timers," Gordon said. "So I don't know a lot about him. It might be he's having trouble getting his feet on the ground after moving here from a big place like Chicago. But I'm a mite put out with him myself."

"Something he's done to you?"

"Oh, no, Miss Starbuck. Far as I know, he's all right, but I don't feel good about him leaving Em's name on his office door instead of scraping it off and putting up his own. It just rubs me the wrong way to see anybody trading on a dead man's good character."

"Perhaps Mr. Perry's just delayed taking care of details like changing the name on his door because he's been too busy getting settled down in a new location," Ki suggested.

"Well, that might be it," Gordon agreed. Turning back to Jessie, he went on, "If you're looking around, figuring you might want to have somebody else handle the Circle Star shipments, I'd appreciate you keeping me in mind, Miss Starbuck."

"I haven't made up my mind about anything like that yet," Jessie said. "But if I do decide to make a change later on, I'll remember you."

"I'd sure appreciate it if you do. I won't act like some of the brokers here and say it don't make any difference who gets your business. I'd like to have it."

"Whether or not I change will depend on a lot of things," Jessie repeated. Then, the tone of her voice casual, she asked, "By the way, did any of the ranchers you do business with have an unusually large number of steers die in the cattle-cars on their way to the yards this year? Or last year either, for that matter?"

"That'd be car-kill you're talking about." Gordon nodded.

"I didn't know you had a name for it," Jessie said. "But I'm sure it means what I think it does—steers that die in the cattle-cars for no apparent reason."

"Yes, ma'am. Car-kill's what we call it. There's almost always a few steers dies on the way from the range to the yards here. Just seems like they can't stand traveling in a cattle-car. No reason anybody's ever been able to figure out. But there's not too many critters that die, maybe one or two out of every hundred head or thereabouts in a good sized shipment."

"Did the ranchers whose cattle you handle have any sizable losses this year?" Jessie asked. Then, before Gordon could answer, she went on quickly, "Or last year, either?"

Gordon shook his head. "Not any more'n usual. I don't seem to recall any of 'em losing over a dozen or so steers."

"I'm sure you'd have heard about it if they had." She went on. "You must pass along information like that to each other."

"Oh, sure. There ain't many secrets around here, Miss Starbuck."

Jessie realized that they'd gotten all the information they could expect from the livestock broker. She said to Ki, "We'd better be getting back to the Exchange. I'd like to find Court Mays before he starts back home."

Making their farewells to Gordon, Jessie and Ki started back to the Exchange Building.

"I suppose you found Mr. Gordon's remarks about carkill as interesting as I did?" Ki asked as they walked slowly through the bright noonday sunshine.

"Very interesting indeed." Jessie nodded. "And he's been here such a long time that he's certainly in a position to know the facts. I think what struck me most was that he didn't say a word about the Circle Star losing so many steers this year."

"I noticed that myself," Ki agreed. "And it's odd that Mr. Pierce didn't seem to've heard about it until you mentioned it to him. Don't you think we'd better do some looking and asking ourselves, Jessie?"

After a moment's thought, Jessie shook her head. "Not yet, Ki. Let's see what kind of news Arthur Pierce has for us first. We can still take things into our own hands if we're not satisfied with whatever he uncovers."

They'd reached the Exchange Building by this time, and when Jessie glanced around the hotel lobby and saw no signs of Court Mays, she stepped up to the desk to ask, "Would you know whether or not Mr. Mays is in his room?"

"Why, Mr. Mays has checked out, Miss Starbuck," the clerk replied. "He received a telegram, and then said that he had to go back to his ranch as fast as he could get there. But he did leave a message for you." Turning, the clerk took an envelope from the pigeonhole assigned to Jessie's room.

Taking the envelope, she stepped aside and opened it. The note in May's sprawling handwriting read:

Sorry I can't stay, Jessie. There's been an accident on the Bar M, and my foreman wired me I'd better hurry back. If you have time and feel like visiting, you've got a standing invitation to the ranch, and if you can't come there this trip, I'll see you at the Circle Star as soon as I can get away.

As she folded the note and returned it to the envelope, Jessie turned to Ki and said, "Court's had to go home; there was an accident of some kind at his ranch. So we'll just go on with our investigation by ourselves."

"What's our next move, then?"

"We'll talk to Arthur Pierce again after lunch, before we make any plans, Ki. Then, depending on what he tells us, we'll decide what we need to do. After what Mr. Gordon told us, I'm more than ever convinced there's something going on that we'd better find out about. And that's what I intend to do, no matter how long we have to stay here."

"I'm not sure what you're going to make of what I've found out, Jessie," Arthur Pierce said as soon as Jessie and Ki had sat down in the chairs he'd drawn up to his desk.

29

"In fact, I'm not really sure what to make of it myself."

"From the frown you're wearing, I get the idea that you're a bit upset," Jessie told him. "And so am I, after a few things that Mr. Gordon mentioned when Ki and I talked to him."

"Whatever Gordon said, Jessie, you can take for gospel truth. If he told me the sun was going to rise in the west tomorrow morning, I'd believe him."

"I think I would, too," she agreed. "He's the same kind of man Emerson White was; you can tell that after you've talked to him a few minutes. I'm sure he's as trustworthy, too. And as for Lucas Perry, as far as Ki and I could find out, he's something of a loner. I got the impression from a few remarks Mr. Gordon made that Perry doesn't mix with the other brokers."

"You said you'd found out something about Perry," Ki said as Jessie paused. "Perhaps Jessie would like to hear what it is before we go any further."

"I've learned a number of very disturbing things, Ki," the Exchange manager replied. "When Emerson White's estate was being settled, his brokerage business was bought by that Chicago outfit, Blossom and Bond. I didn't know anything about them so I wired a friend of mine who's on the Chicago Livestock Board asking for what he could tell me. Since they'd notified us that Lucas Perry was coming from Chicago to handle Emerson's office, I asked about him, too."

"And your friend in Chicago gave them a clean bill of health?" Jessie asked when Pierce paused for breath.

"He did as far as Blossom and Bond's concerned. They're primarily commodities brokers, though; their main business is wheat. As for Perry, his name's on the list of commodities brokers working out of the Blossom and

30

Bond office, but my friend didn't know anything about him."

"Then he's not really licensed as a livestock broker?" Jessie frowned.

"That's the only conclusion I could come to." Pierce nodded. "I've sent a telegram to Blossom and Bond, but haven't had an answer yet. Maybe I'll know more when I hear from them."

"Just how important is this license you've mentioned?" Ki asked. "Do the men who get one have to pass tests, or something like that?"

"There's a long form they have to fill out when they apply for recognition by the Exchange," Pierce told him. "You know yourself, Jessie, how important a broker is to you ranchers. We've got to be sure that we're not getting a bunch of brokers who don't know which end of a steer has horns. But there are some questions in the form that help us to screen out cheats and crooks."

"I think I know what you're about to tell us next," Jessie said when Pierce paused. "When you started asking questions the people in your office couldn't find Perry's admission form."

"That's right," the Exchange manager admitted. "We gave him permission to use Em White's office temporarily because Blossom and Bond had bought the brokerage license from Em's estate. My clerk remembers giving Perry the questionnaire, but it seems that he's never filled it out and returned it."

"How could something like that have gone on for almost two years without being noticed?" Jessie frowned.

Pierce shrugged. "It's one of those things that happen in any office, Jessie. Everybody thought someone else had taken care of what's usually just a routine matter."

"What do you intend to do next?" Jessie asked, then

added quickly, "Or suggest that I do? We won't be shipping another herd to market for quite a while, but if my suspicions are correct, this Lucas Perry has stolen a lot of money from me with falsified reports, so I don't want to waste any time getting this mix-up straightened out."

"And I want to help you," Pierce said quickly. "Letting something like this happen doesn't do the Exchange any good."

Jessie shook her head. "The people in your office couldn't help knowing about an investigation you began, Arthur. These stockyards are like a small town; everybody knows what's going on. And if word leaked back to Perry, it might give him time to cover his tracks. Give Ki and me a day or so to look into this a little deeper before you get involved."

"If that's how you want to handle it, I won't object," Pierce said, nodding. "I'll keep things quiet for right now. But sooner or later, the Exchange will have to move in."

"Of course," Jessie agreed. "I wouldn't have it any other way. But as far as we know now, the Circle Star's the only ranch involved, though I'm sure we'll find out there are some others that Perry's victimized."

"I hope not," Pierce told her. "One swindle at a time is about all the Exchange can stand."

"We'll be very quiet and discreet," Jessie promised. "All I want is to get back the money Perry's stolen from the Circle Star with those faked cattle-death reports. Once I can prove that everything Ki and I have uncovered is true, I'm sure the head office in Chicago will make good the loss and see that Perry goes to jail for embezzling."

"Take whatever time you need, Jessie," Pierce said. "I'm sure the Exchange will look a little bit foolish when the whole story comes out, but we'll manage to survive that."

"Ki and I have already started digging," Jessie went on. "And we'll work as fast as we can."

Ki said thoughtfully, "We have one big problem to solve first, Jessie—the information we need that Perry claims he's sent to the Blossom and Bond office in Chicago."

"Yes," Jessie agreed. She turned back to Pierce. "He's promised to write Chicago and ask them to send it back here, but after hearing what you've just said, I have an idea that he didn't have any intention of doing that."

"Perhaps if I wired the Chicago Livestock Board, they can get the information for me from the brokerage house," Pierce suggested. "It's worth a try."

"Almost anything's worth a try," Jessie agreed. "You take care of that, Arthur. In the meantime, Ki and I will see what we can pry out of Lucas Perry."

When Jessie and Ki returned to Perry's office, it was closed.

"Do you think he's skipped out?" Ki asked. "He might have, you know. After we showed up at his office he may have thought we knew he'd falsified those car-kills and started running away from trouble."

"I don't know what to think, Ki, and I'd hesitate to make a guess. He may have had some business to take care of downtown in Fort Worth, and that's quite a distance from the Exchange. It'd take him a while to go there and get back."

"And he might have gone home," Ki suggested, "sick or something."

"I know one thing," Jessie said determinedly. "I'm not going to let him get away from us if I can help it. Suppose

33

we split up. You go to Perry's flat and see if he's there and just decided to leave early today. I'll stay here in case he shows up."

"And if he's at his apartment?" Ki asked.

"If you can persuade him to come back to the yards with you, I'll be here watching. If he doesn't want to come here, send your hackman back for me and I'll join you at his flat."

Ki nodded. "Fair enough. We'll find him, no matter where he is. And if he's not at his flat, I'll wait a little while. If he doesn't show up in half an hour or so, I'll ask the landlord for some hints where he might be, then try to find him if I get any ideas."

"Unless Perry's panicked and skipped the country, he'll have to show up here or at his flat sometime soon," Jessie said. "All we've got to do is be patient."

After Ki had gone, Jessie brushed off the steps leading up to the door of Perry's office and sat down to wait. As the day had heated up, the odor of the stockyards had grown stronger; but the smell of manure, both stale and fresh, was one to which Jessie had become accustomed on the Circle Star. She sat patiently, watching the activities in the yards while the midday sun peaked.

Jessie had not really realized until now how big an enterprise the Exchange was. Its stockpens had been laid out in a rough rectangle, one end extending for a half-mile along the north bank of the Trinity River and stretching for more than two miles across the gently rolling prairie. The yards were made up of scores of small individual pens that would accommodate ten or fifteen head of cattle and dozens of larger pens, some big enough to confine a sizable herd.

Wide alleyways separated the pens, and the tracks of the I and GN Railroad ran the length of the yards. On them the

34

cattle-cars sat, waiting to be unloaded and then reloaded almost at once and shipped to the slaughterhouses to which the steers had been sold by the brokers. There was always some kind of activity in the wide alleyways. The yard cowboys were busy chousing small groups of steers—too small to be call herds—from one of the square pens to another, unloading a cattle-car at one point along the tracks and at another point loading one with a bunch made up for the brokers' shipments.

Jessie had been waiting for almost two hours when Ki came back. "I didn't have any luck at all," he said. "And since you're still waiting too, I'm sure yours was the same."

"Well, Perry can't have just disappeared," Jessie told him. "Let's go and get some food and then come back here and wait. It's tiresome, but it's the only thing I can see to do."

Although they waited patiently after a fast luncheon until the sun had dropped to the horizon, Lucas Perry did not appear at the brokerage office.

"We'll have supper and then go to his flat," Jessie told Ki as they started toward the Exchange Building in the reddening light of sunset. "He's sure to be at his flat sometime tonight."

Pushing aside their discouragement, Jessie and Ki ate at the Exchange restaurant, then in a rented livery rig went to check Perry's flat. Their knocks brought no response; nor did Perry show up after they'd waited until almost midnight.

"He's managed to dodge us today," Jessie told Ki as they separated in the hallway at the doors of their rooms. "But tomorrow's another day, and we're sure to find him then."

35

"Suppose we don't?" Ki asked. "Suppose he really has gone on the dodge?"

"As angry as I am now, I'm just in a mood to try to find him here in Fort Worth for one more day," she replied. "Then we'll take the first train to Chicago and go to the head office of that brokerage house he's working for. It's not just the fact that Perry's stolen almost sixty thousand dollars from the Circle Star, Ki. If we let him get away, he'll go somewhere else and find another cattle rancher to victimize. But we'll try again, and wait to decide exactly what we'll do if we don't find him tomorrow."

She went into her room, angry and a bit dispirited. Lighting the lamp that stood on the bureau, Jessie stepped over to the luggage stand that held her suitcase and began looking for the dressing gown that she'd been too busy to unpack the evening before.

She straightened up when she turned away from the luggage rack, and a flicker of movement behind the lace curtains at the window caught her eye. The years she and Ki had spent in constant danger of attack from hired killers sent by the European cartel had sharpened Jessie's reflexes to a razor's edge. She gave no indication that she'd seen anything unusual, but turned back to the suitcase and bent over it again as though she was looking for something she'd forgotten.

Her holstered Colt was tucked into one corner of the bag and she closed her hand around its butt. Instead of straightening up again, she dropped to the floor, flicking the Colt to free it from its holster.

A shot sounded outside the window an instant before the leather holster dropped off the gun and Jessie could bring the Colt around to fire. The tinkle of shattering glass mixed with the echoes of the shot fired by the man on the ledge outside her window; then the small, high-pitched sounds were drowned by the bark of Jessie's weapon.

She kept her eyes on the black square that now showed behind the fluttering curtains, but the vague silhouetted form she'd seen on the ledge had vanished. Jessie rolled to the window with her Colt ready to find a target, and kept herself prone on the floor as she raised her head cautiously to peer into the blackness outside, but the half-visible figure of the man she'd seen on the ledge had vanished.

Chapter 4

A tapping on the panel of the door leading to the hall broke the silence that had followed the two shots. Jessie paid no attention to it. She was at the window now, parting the breeze-billowed curtains to look out. A glance into the darkness along the building's wall showed her that there was no one perched on the ornamental ledge of whitish limestone that girdled the second floor of the building. The tapping was repeated, but now Jessie was straining her eyes, trying to pierce the blackness that veiled the ground below her window.

She thought for a moment that she saw a sprawled form lying beside the building's wall, but could not be sure. The tapping sounded at the door, sharper and more urgent than before. Jessie turned away from the window and unlocked the door. In the corridor outside, Ki was twisting the door knob even while the rasp of the key Jessie turned had died away. In the distance she could hear the sound of voices.

Ki slipped into the room and closed the door quickly. He asked, "Are you all right, Jessie?"

"Yes. Whoever shot at me missed. I got a glimpse of movement outside the window and dropped to the floor before he could fire."

"Did you get a look at whoever it was?"

Jessie shook her head. "No. All I could see was someone moving outside the window. It was so dark that I couldn't tell whether it was a man or a woman, but something gave me the impression it was a man."

Ki had crossed to the window while they were talking. He leaned out, peering toward the ground. After a moment he straightened up and shook his head.

"I can't see the ground, either." He broke off as someone in the corridor knocked at the door. Looking at Jessie, he raised his eyebrows questioningly.

"Oh, we'll have to open the door," Jessie told him. "I'm sure it's somebody from the hotel, wanting to find out about the shooting."

"What will you tell them?"

"Why, exactly what happened, of course, but without going into too much detail," Jessie replied. "Now, no burglar is going to shoot anybody unless he's cornered trying to get away from someone. You and I are sure that this attack has something to do with Perry and the cattle he stole from the Circle Star herd, but the only fact we really know is that there was a man outside who took a shot at me through the window."

Ki nodded, then opened the door. A wide-chested man with a deputy sheriff's star pinned on his shirt pocket stood in the doorway. He carried a dark lantern in one hand, a revolver in the other. Behind him in the hall a small group of people, a half dozen men and two or three women, stood talking excitedly.

40

"Who was it doing the shooting up here?" the deputy asked, looking from Ki to Jessie. His attention was caught at once by the Colt in Jessie's hand. "Was it you, ma'am?"

"Yes." Jessie nodded. "But I only fired one shot. I saw a man outside my window. I was standing by my suitcase over there and had my gun in my hand when I saw him. He fired just a second or two before I did. He missed, but I think I hit him."

"Do you, now," the deputy grunted skeptically. Pushing past Jessie and Ki, he went to the window and thrust his lantern out to look at the ledge. He peered to the right and left, then leaned out, gazing at the ground. Straightening up as he turned away from the window, he went on, "Looks like you really did hit him, ma'am. There's blood spots on that ledge outside. It's too dark to see the ground, though. Guess I'll have to go downstairs and find out if you got him good enough to keep him from getting away."

By this time the crowd in the hall had doubled in number. A man at the back was trying to push through to the door. Jessie could not see his face but she recognized his voice when he raised it. The newcomer was Arthur Pierce.

"Let me through, please! I'm the manager of the Exchange, and I'm asking you now to go back to your rooms, or down to the lobby. If any of you know anything about those shots, I'll want to talk with you later."

Like trickles of cold molasses spreading over a pancake, the people crammed into the corridor began moving. Pierce got to the door of Jessie's room at last and looked from her and Ki to the deputy.

"Are you all right, Jessie?" he asked.

"Just fine, Arthur. And so is Ki."

With a nod, Pierce turned to the guard and asked, "Well, Sullivan, what happened?"

41

"Seems like somebody got on that trim ledge outside and took a shot at this lady though the window," the man answered. He jerked a thumb toward Jessie and added, "That's what she says, anyways. And she didn't say who it was outside."

"Whatever she said, you can bet it's true, Sullivan," Pierce said sharply. "This lady's Miss Jessica Starbuck, and she happens to own one of the biggest cattle ranches in the state of Texas." He turned to Jessie as he went on, "Sullivan's in charge of the stockyards guards, Jessie. He's also a special deputy sheriff in Tarrant County." Addressing Sullivan again, he went on, "Now, I'm sure that Miss Starbuck's interested in knowing who shot at her, and so am I."

"I guess I better go downstairs and see if she hit whoever it was outside there, then," Sullivan said. "There's blood on the ledge outside, so I reckon the lady scored a hit."

"Dammit, man, you should've gone downstairs at once!" Pierce snapped. "Now, I want to know how that fellow got on the Exchange grounds and up on that ledge! I want to know where the outside guards were and why they didn't stop him!"

"Yessir." Sullivan nodded. "I was getting ready to go downstairs and take a look around."

After his sudden outburst, Pierce's anger subsided. His voice was again in control as he told the man, "I'm sure you can believe whatever Miss Starbuck told you. And if she did hit whoever was on that ledge, he's probably somewhere close by. We'd better go outside and look around the grounds. Bring your lantern and come along."

"Do you mind if Ki and I go with you?" Jessie asked quickly. "After all, I was the one that man was aiming at."

"Come along by all means, Jessie," Pierce replied.

42

"You're the only one who saw him. He might've been hit so badly that he can't move. If he's still there, alive or dead, maybe you can identify him for the police."

"I'm afraid that even if I saw that man again I wouldn't recognize him," Jessie told Pierce as they started for the stairway. "I never did get a good look at him. All I could see at first was that someone was outside the window looking at me. I'd just taken my Colt out of my suitcase and had it in my hand, and when I saw the glinting of light from his gun I fired through the window as I was dropping to the floor. He shot at almost the same time. Of course, the glass in the window smashed when our bullets hit it. Then the curtains began blowing, and I couldn't see anything at all outside."

"If he's gotten away, I'm afraid it's partly my fault," Ki put in. "If I'd gone after the fellow as soon as I'd found out that Jessie wasn't hurt I might have caught him."

"Don't blame yourself for that, Ki," Jessie said. "Unless my shot crippled him, he'd've been gone before you could've gotten downstairs."

They reached the lobby and started around the Exchange Building. The dark lantern carried by Sullivan gave a dim light at best, but it was enough to enable them to walk rapidly around the building and reach the corner below Jessie's window. Light still streamed through the glassless sash, and combined with the lantern's glow it brightened the ground enough to be reflected in the smear of blood on the ground where the would-be killer had landed, and to enable them to follow his trail of blood drops away from the hotel.

After they'd left the area brightened by the windows, keeping to the blood-trail became increasingly difficult. Time after time they were forced to zigzag through the calf-deep grass to spot the small droplets that still clung to the tips of the dried grass and weeds. The trail straightened out after they'd covered a few hundred yards, and led them along the edge of the pebbled road to the bridge over Marine Creek.

Once across the bridge and on Main Street the trail of the fleeing shootist became even more difficult to follow. Only an occasional pinpoint of blood shining in the yellow dust when the gleam of the lantern struck it gave them any hint that they were still heading in the right direction.

"We're all right as long as he keeps bleeding," Ki observed as they moved slowly forward behind the guard, whose swinging lantern picked up the glistening drops.

"There ain't much place for him to go but to town," Sullivan said. "He's carrying a piece of lead in him, so he's most likely heading for one of the joints down in the district where he can hole up and find somebody who'll fix up that bullet hole without nobody asking him any questions."

"I think you're probably right," Jessie agreed. "If we lose the trail, do you know the best places to look for him?"

"Why, sure, ma'am," the man answered. "Before the sheriff taken me on for a deputy, I was on the Fort Worth police force."

"You'd know, then," she said, and nodded. "Where would you start looking?"

"Now, that's hard to say, Miss Starbuck. The Mansion Saloon's got what they call a rooming house attached to it, and so has the El Paso. Then there's the Virginia House and—well, a bunch more like them. They're all places where nobody asks questions if a man comes in bleeding from a bullet hole, as long as he's got cash money in his pocket."

"Which of them would the man we're looking for be most likely to go to?" she persisted.

44

"I'll say right off that none of them is places where I'd take a lady, Miss Starbuck. But me and Mr. Pierce or your man Ki can—"

Jessie broke in to say, "Forget that I'm wearing a skirt instead of trousers, and take us to the nearest one of those places you mentioned."

"I guess it ain't my place to argue," Sullivan acquiesced. "So if you say so, we might as well head for the Virginia House. It's the biggest crook hangout I know about, and besides, it's the closest."

After the stockyards and the Livestock Exchange had been formed, and a second railroad had pushed its main line into town, Fort Worth had become Texas's biggest cattle-shipping center. Even though the night was well along by now, the streets were still busy as their guide led them off Commerce Street and into the older section of town.

Here the dark windows of expansive houses built during the period of the early cattle barons predominated, although most of their original owners had moved away long ago. Saloons had taken over almost all the corners; at many intersections four drinking places showed lights at the tops and bottoms of batwing doors. The houses that faced the street between the corners were gracious old dwellings, most of them two stories high. Only a few of them showed lights around the edges of drawn shades or through cracks between the slats of closed shutters.

There were still some pedestrians abroad in spite of the late hour. Most of them were men who kept close to the shadows of the buildings, and few of them looked at the strangely-assorted quartet with the Exchange guard in the lead that was making its way along the uneven brick sidewalk.

"How much farther is it to this place you're taking us?" Pierce asked Sullivan as they stepped off the sidewalk at one of the rare corners brightened by a streetlight.

"Not far, Mr. Pierce. It's the house just past that saloon catty-cornered from us over yonder."

When the guard raised his arm to point, a shot rang out and red muzzle-blast broke the dark shadow which veiled the front porch of the big house they were approaching.

A man ran out of the gloom that hid the facade of the house. He started running diagonally across the intersection, stopped when he reached the brick walkway on the opposite side, and turned long enough to let off another shot. Sullivan yelped in pain and began tottering backward, his arms flailing the air as he sought to stay on his feet.

Jessie had drawn her Colt when the first shot sounded, but the guard's staggering move placed him between her and the man who'd shot him. She stepped to one side, looking for the man who'd run from the shadows, but he'd already run into the deep shadow cast by the houses on the opposite side of the intersection.

From somewhere close by the shrill blast of a police whistle cut through the dark night air. Jessie was halfway across the intersection by now, with Ki running a short distance to one side of her. Both of them were heading for the shadows that had swallowed up the fleeing men.

"Be careful, Jessie!" Ki called to her. "He can see us, but we can't see him!"

"We've got to get closer to see him!" she replied.

"But we're not even sure he's the man we're after!"

"He must've recognized us or he wouldn't've shot at us when he saw us in the streetlight!" Jessie replied without slowing down.

Another police whistle, further away than the first, shrilled on one of the dark side streets. The distant grating thuds of running feet on the graveled streets added an undertone to the sudden noises that had broken the night's stillness.

Jessie and Ki had now gotten beyond the area illuminated by the streetlight, but they could still hear the scraping thunks of the fleeing man's feet ahead of them. Keeping in the center of the dark street, they ran on.

Ki called, "He's just ahead of us, Jessie!"

Jessie strained her eyes peering into the blackness, but could see nothing except the lines of light escaping from the shuttered front windows of one of the houses ahead. Then the lighted grid was broken by a black shadow, and she fired, trying to gauge the man's location in the distance.

No cry broke the air following her shot, and she knew that she'd missed. She realized, too, that she now had only three cartridges left in her Colt, and no spare shells for the weapon. The unexpected attack on her at the hotel followed by the swiftly unfolding chase of which she was now a part had given her no opportunity to put extra ammunition into her pocket.

Jessie could still hear the sounds of the running fugitive ahead her, but Ki's soft sandals made no noise even on the graveled street. Though she knew that he'd gotten ahead of her in their pursuit, she could no longer pinpoint his location either by sight or by sound in the dense darkness.

In the gloom of the street ahead she saw a black shadow break the feeble glow that filtered through the shaded windows of another house far in front of her. Instinctively she raised her Colt, but the shadow had passed before she could find the blur of movement in her gunsight, and she had no idea whether she'd seen the fugitive or whether the running man was Ki. She lowered the Colt's muzzle and kept running.

Somewhere ahead of her another police whistle shrilled,

47

but Jessie could not locate its source. Behind her she heard one of the Forth Worth policeman call to his companion, and she realized belatedly that she'd been moving through the gloom faster than they had.

Far ahead, another streetlight glowed, but its rays did nothing to lighten the gloom through which Jessie was running. Then she saw a shadowy form break the light, but again the gloom returned so quickly that she could not tell whether the figure of which she'd gotten such a momentary glimpse was that of Ki or of some stranger.

She stopped for a moment, not to catch her breath, but to keep from making any noise herself while she listened for the thud of footsteps that might give her a clue as to who was where. All that Jessie heard was the continuing scraping of feet on the gravel surface of the midnight-black street.

Unexpectedly, a glimmer of light broke the darkness of the street just ahead of her. It was followed by a shot that loosed a spurt of muzzle-blast from the street between Jessie and the glowing beams that were showing farther down the thoroughfare. Spurred by both training and habit, Jessie brought up the muzzle of her Colt. She knew that the moving man was not Ki, for Ki never carried firearms, but caution warned her that one or both of the Fort Worth policemen might have managed to pass her in the darkness. The thought kept her finger from squeezing the trigger. The light-rays in front of her were so far away that they showed her nothing except a moving blur. She still was unable to identify the blurred black silhouette.

She moved forward cautiously when the dark shadow stopped. The dim light that had showed farther along on the street was moving now, coming toward Jessie. She could see the vague outline of the man ahead of her, but despite her familiarity with Ki's stocky figure she could not tell whether it was him or the man they were chasing.

Her slow, cautious advance had taken her only a few steps when her foot grated loudly on a patch of loose gravel. The light that had showed ahead was suddenly extinguished, but not before the silhouetted form of the man ahead of her moved quickly and the gun he'd raised broke the darkness of the street again with a red jet of muzzle-blast as the loud report of his shot shattered the quietness.

Knowing now that the form ahead of her was neither Ki nor one of the Fort Worth officers from whom she'd pulled away in the darkness, Jessie fired at the blurred shadow in the blackness. The report of her Colt was echoed by a second shot from someone else, someone ahead of her on the opposite side of the street.

A third shot cracked from the gun held by the man who Jessie was now certain had been the quarry of the chase through the midnight-black streets. The report sounded before the echoes of the other shots had died away, but the angle of the jetting muzzle-blast told Jessie that the gun was sagging in the dying shooter's hand. The red blast spurted downward, toward the ground at his feet.

"Hold your fire, whoever you are!" Jessie called into the blackness. "And if you've got matches or a night lantern, show a light!"

For an interminable moment, Jessie waited for her command to be obeyed. Then the glow of a lighted match broke the darkness across the street and shone for a moment before a brighter light replaced it: the whitish glowing illumination that could come only from an acetylene lantern.

A man's voice sounded behind the light as Jessie blinked in the brilliance of its rays, and the speaker called, "Who in hell are you, lady?"

49

"My name's Jessica Starbuck," she replied. "Are you a policeman?"

"Sure am."

"Then be careful with your gun! There are some other people moving around here in the dark!"

"Listen to her, Clancey!" a third voice called. "Me and Sam are out here!"

"And so am I!" Ki said loudly. His voice came from the darkness before he walked into the arc of light now cast by the lantern the policeman was holding. "I've been trying to capture that man, too. He tried to kill Miss Starbuck just a little while ago."

"Where in hell— Excuse me, lady," one of the officers began. Before he could go on, footsteps grated on the graveled street and the man holding the light raised it to reveal Arthur Pierce, running and puffing as he hurried to join them.

"Sorry I—fell—behind," Pierce panted. "I stayed a minute with Sullivan to be sure he was all right; then, when I started running, I'm so soft from deskwork that I couldn't catch up with you any faster."

"Well, now that you're here," Jessie said, "and we have some policemen around, let's see if we can find out who the man was who started all this trouble."

★

Chapter 5

"I'm as curious as anybody to learn who he is, Jessie," Arthur Pierce said. "But isn't that a job for the police?"

"Of course," Jessie agreed. "But right now we're pretty sure this fellow's the one who tried to kill me, and I'm curious to know more about him. I intend to be standing right behind the police, looking over their shoulders while they're finding out."

Ki had been listening to their conversation. Now he asked Jessie, "We're going with them to headquarters, then?"

"Headquarters, or the morgue, if Fort Worth has one," she replied. "I want to know whether this man was working alone or if he might have some friends with the same idea he had of putting a bullet into me."

"I don't suppose any of us doubts that he's the same one," Ki agreed. "And I'm just as curious as you are to find out why he was after you."

"We sure don't aim to keep any secrets from you or Mr. Pierce, ma'am," one of the Fort Worth policemen said quickly. "But if this fellow's not one of our local badmen, it might take us the rest of the night or even longer to find out who he is and where he's from."

"You do intend to do that, though?" Jessie asked.

"Oh, sure we do. But right now you've had a real exciting time, and I bet you're tired out. Why don't you go back to the Exchange with Mr. Pierce and get a good night's rest? If you'll come downtown again tomorrow morning and stop in at headquarters, we'll know a lot more than we do now."

"That makes good sense, Jessie," Pierce put in. "If you want me or Sullivan to come with you tomorrow, I'll be glad to, and I'm sure he would."

"Thanks, Arthur, but Ki will be with me tomorrow," Jessie replied. "I suppose I am a little bit too impatient. We'll find a hackney and go back to the Exchange. And don't worry about coming to town with us in the morning. We're used to handling our own problems."

"So far, all we've been able to find out for sure about that fellow who shot at you is that he's not one of our local badmen, and he's been going by the name of Lipsey the little time he's been here," the sergeant told Jessie and Ki when they arrived at Fort Worth Police Headquarters the next morning.

"And how long a time is that?" Jessie asked.

"About a year and a half is the best guess we can make," the officer replied.

"He's been in trouble before then?"

"No, ma'am, Miss Starbuck. At least not none we've dug up yet. But that ain't to say he might not've been up to some kind of crookedness we haven't caught up with."

"And he hasn't made any close friends—what crooks call 'a connection'?" Ki asked.

"Oh, he's said hello to a lot of bad ones, especially the ones that hang out in the saloons along Twenty-fourth Street. Which is sorta funny, because he's been renting a room at the Virginia House. I guess you've heard somebody mention it. It passes as a rooming house, but it's really more of a—"

When the policeman stopped short, Jessie picked up the descriptive thread he'd left dangling. "A brothel," she said. "The sort of place that your official records call a house of prostitution."

"That's right, ma'am. The Virginia House ain't the kind of place a lady like you would want to stay at."

"But it's very close to where we caught up with him last night," Jessie pointed out. Then she went on, "So you're really not sure of anything much about him, are you?"

"Well, we know it was a slug from a forty-five that killed him," the man answered. "And he had a bullet-hole in his left arm that came from somebody's gun."

"I'm reasonably sure that was from the shot I fired at him through the window of my room at the Exchange Hotel," Jessie said. "I was taking my Colt out of my suitcase and had it in my hand when I saw him at the window."

"You didn't miss finishing him by much, then," the office said. "The hole was in his upper arm about even with his chest." He frowned thoughtfully as he went on, "Oh, yes. There's one more thing that might make you feel easier about shooting him. He was a big-city crook. We're right certain about that."

"How can you be so sure?"

Before answering her, the sergeant opened a drawer of his desk and took out a bulky, bulging manila envelope. He opened its clasped top and dumped the contents on his desktop. The most prominent items were a blue-steel revolver and a bulky wallet, but there was also a small sum of money, several unfired shells, and a few scraps of paper.

Lifting the pistol from the litter that had fallen on his desk, the officer held it out for Jessie to inspect. She looked at it closely, then looked up at the sergeant.

"Perhaps this gun tells you something," she said. "But all I can see is that it's a Colt revolver. Anybody can buy a gun of this kind almost anywhere."

"That's right, ma'am," he agreed. "But look close at the caliber." He flipped a swiveled locking-catch below the hammer and tipped the cylinder and barrel down. Pointing to the small cylinder orifices, he went on, "I guess you know enough about guns to tell what caliber it is?"

"I'd say a twenty-two." Jessie frowned. "Not a heavy enough slug to do much harm, unless it's in the hands of an expert shot."

"Seems like you know more about guns than I figured." The sergeant smiled. "And you're right. Now, what I'm getting at is that this little gun's what the Colt people call a Pocket Revolver, and what a lot of other folks call a Baby Colt. But what I'm getting at is it's the kind of gun crooks in big towns like New York and Chicago and St. Louis favor. It'll shoot truer and give a man more rounds than a derringer, and it don't make much of a bulge in the kind of tight clothes city folks wear."

"That's good reasoning, sergeant," Jessie said thoughtfully. "You wouldn't like to make another guess, about which city this Lipsey came from, I suppose?"

"St. Louis, maybe. Or it could be Chicago. They're the big towns closest to us here."

Jessie and Ki exchanged glances. Then Jessie turned back to the sergeant and said, "Well, you've been very helpful, and I appreciate it. You know where I'm staying,

54

and if you run across any more information that I might be interested in, I'd like to have it."

"Count on us, Miss Starbuck. We'll pass on anything else we figure you might want to hear about."

Leaving police headquarters, Jessie told Ki, "It's still early. We'll get a hack and stop by Lucas Perry's flat on our way back to the Exchange. There's a chance that we might catch him before he leaves for his office."

"He's certainly keeping out of sight," Ki commented. Then he asked thoughtfully, "Do you think he might've skipped out?"

Jessie nodded. "That's a possibility, of course. And the longer he avoids us, the more positive I get that he's been swindling not only the Circle Star but other ranchers as well. If we don't find him at home this time, we'll watch his office today. If he still hasn't shown up, I think it's safe to assume that he's run away."

As Jessie and Ki settled back on the seat of the hackney cab she said to Ki, "I've been thinking about Perry and that Chicago brokerage house he works for. Did you get the same idea I did when that policeman was talking about the gun this fellow Lipsey was carrying?"

"I thought it was an odd choice of pistol for a man on the wrong side of the law to be carrying," Ki replied. "Then I remembered that Lipsey was a city crook."

"Of course. He wouldn't be trying to knock a man out of the saddle at long range with his revolver. He'd be aiming at a closer target."

"A twenty-two will kill somebody just as dead as a forty-five will, if whoever pulls the trigger is a good shot," Ki reminded her.

"Of course it will." Jessie nodded. "And when the officer mentioned where crooks use those little pistols—"

Ki finished the remark for her. "Chicago was one of the

places he mentioned where guns like that are common. And while the sergeant was talking to you about the pistol, I realized that while he was busy educating you about guns, I had a chance to take a quick look at what the police found in Lipsey's pockets."

"And found what?"

"A wallet with some money in it, but not a great amount. Part of a plug of chewing tobacco. Extra shells for his pistol."

"I was hoping you'd found something interesting."

"Perhaps I did. There were two things I haven't mentioned yet that I slipped in my pocket while the sergeant was giving you a lesson in firearms."

Ki reached into the capacious pocket of his loosely-fitting blouse and took out two small objects, which he handed to Jessie. She frowned as she looked at them lying in her opened palm. One was a copper disc the size of a half-dollar, the other a square of tightly folded paper. She picked up the disc first, and as she studied the embossed inscription on it a frown puckered her face. She looked up at Ki.

"All that's on this is 'Masie. One free. Two-ten Harrison Street Court,'" she said. "It doesn't mean a thing to me, Ki, but I think it's one of those tokens that prostitutes in the red-light districts give their good customers to bring them back. Am I right?"

"Completely." Ki nodded. "But that's not the most interesting thing about the token, Jessie. It's something that you might expect to find a man like Lipsey carrying around."

"Why did you take it, then? We're not interested in what his morals might've been."

"You're not one of the disadvantaged, Jessie. My countrymen are; they have to live in some undesirable neigh-

56

borhoods, as you should know from seeing the Oriental colony in San Francisco."

"I'm still at sea, Ki," she told him.

"When I visited Chicago with Alex for the first time, I was interested in finding some Orientals to talk with," Ki went on. "When I explored the Chicago slums, Harrison Street Court was one of the streets I encountered. I remember it very well, even today."

"Now I understand!" Jessie exclaimed. "The token proves that if Lipsey didn't live in Chicago, he spent some time there. And Lucas Perry worked for a brokerage house in Chicago before he came here to Fort Worth!"

Ki nodded. "Exactly."

"I suppose that's as close as we can come to proving there's a connection between them," she said thoughtfully. "And even if it satisfies us, I don't think it'd be accepted as evidence in a court of law."

"Perhaps not," Ki said. "But you haven't looked at that piece of paper yet."

Jessie unfolded the tightly crimped wad. It was the thin, yellowish paper that was commonplace in telegraph offices. She'd gotten enough telegrams on business affairs to recognize its origin. When she spread the paper and smoothed it out she could see that it was only a strip torn from a larger sheet. It bore only a few words, written in the flowing round script favored universally by telegraphers: *Cancel S account.*

"Do you have any idea what it means?" she asked, looking at Ki, a puzzled frown on her face.

He shook his head. "Nothing I can be sure of, Jessie. I've been juggling it around in my mind since I glanced at it while you and the police sergeant were talking. That's one reason I kept it—that and the thought I had that it wasn't the kind of thing you'd expect to find in a wallet that belonged to a man like Lipsey."

"If it wasn't something important to him, he wouldn't have folded it up the way it was, and tucked it away in his wallet," Jessie went on, talking to herself as much as to Ki.

"I'm sure you recognize where it came from," he suggested.

"Of course. It's been torn off a telegraph message. Goodness knows I've gotten enough of them from—" She broke off and looked at the scrap of paper again. Then she went on, "Brokerage offices use the telegraph a great deal, Ki."

"Yes, that thought occurred to me, just as it has to you," he agreed.

"And the S could mean a stockbroker's abbreviation for an account, or it could mean—" She stopped short.

Ki and Jessie had been through so many crises together that they could almost communicate without speaking. He said, "Your thought's right on the mark, Jessie. It could also mean Starbuck. That could be a note from Lucas Perry to Lipsey. He'd have telegraph blanks in his office; all brokers do these days."

Jessie nodded, then picked up the thought that had popped into her mind the instant that she saw the cryptic message. "It might be from a telegram as well, Ki. An order from Perry's boss in Chicago. I know that if I got a telegraph message that might be used against me in court, I'd be sure to tear off my name and address before I let go of it."

"Well, neither of us is likely to worry about our messages winding up as evidence in a trial. Lucas Perry would, though, if he's the kind of man the evidence we've gathered so far indicates that he is."

"It's a thin tie, Ki." Jessie frowned. "But it's very hard

58

to forge a telegram, and I think it's all we need. You and I have had enough experience with criminals to know that there aren't very many lone wolves left among them."

Ki frowned. "A gang, you think?"

"Perhaps not in the sense you're suggesting. But I can imagine a crooked brokerage house that finds it's handy sometimes to have a burglar or even a killer on the payroll."

Their conversation was interrupted as the hackie reined up in front of the block of flats in which Lucas Perry lived.

"I'll go knock on his door," Ki volunteered. "If he still doesn't answer, and we don't find him in his office when we get to the stockyards, we can be pretty sure that something very fishy is going on."

Ki stepped out of the hack and vanished into the building. He was gone for only a few minutes, and emerged shaking his head when he saw Jessie watching from the window of the hack.

"No answer to my knocks," he reported.

"I was pretty sure there wouldn't be," Jessie replied. "If we don't find him in his office, I think it's safe to assume he's run away." As Ki settled into the seat beside her and the hackie reined the vehicle into motion, she went on, "Now that we've found out that the man who I'm sure now has cheated me and the man who shot at me are both from the same place, it puts an entirely different light on this situation."

"Yes. I've been thinking pretty much the same thing."

Jessie went on, "Unless I've forgotten my geography, here in Fort Worth we're very nearly halfway from the Circle Star to Chicago."

"You sound like you're thinking about going the rest of the way and checking up on the outfit Lucas Perry works for."

"I'm thinking very seriously of doing just that, unless we manage to find Perry and he can satisfy me about those steers that he claims died on the way here from the ranch. There are crooks in the brokerage business, just like there are rustlers on the prairie, Ki. But we've still got some questions to ask before we can be sure."

"We'll have to find Perry before you can ask him anything. After you talked to him the first time, he's done a pretty good job of dodging you," Ki pointed out. "He certainly acts like he's got something to hide."

"Yes. And I don't have much use for a man who avoids talking to me, even if I do suspect that all I'll hear from him is a pack of lies."

Jessie broke off as the hack-driver pulled up at the hotel entrance. After they'd paid the driver and were starting into the sprawling red brick building she picked up the conversation where she'd left off.

"We'll give Perry one more day, Ki. Let's divide our time and watch his office every minute. If he still doesn't show up before evening, then we'll decide what we should do next."

Chapter 6

"I think it's an odds-on bet by now that Perry's not going to show up at all today, Ki," Jessie said as she tried to stretch while still sitting down.

"You may be right. If he came here at all, it was while we were downtown at police headquarters."

Jessie was sitting on the ground, while Ki was hunkered down on his heels. He showed no signs of strain, though he'd been in much the same posture since he and Jessie had begun their watch in mid-morning, after their fruitless visit to Perry's flat. They'd found that the only place where they could watch the door of Perry's brokerage office door was some fifty or sixty yards from the office door, at the back of an empty stock-pen beside the railroad spur used to shunt cattle-cars into the yards for loading and unloading.

It was not an ideal spot for a prolonged watch. They'd been forced to take cover under the thick board chute that slanted up from ground level at the stock-pen gate and rose to span the space between the ground and the bottoms of the cattle-car doors, some three feet above the tracks. The cramped triangular space below the chute was barely wide enough to conceal both Jessie and Ki, and even its greatest height at the level of a cattle-car's sliding doors was too low to allow them to stand erect.

"There's a pretty good chance that Perry heard about Lipsey getting killed by the police last night," Ki went on. "And if he did, he may have panicked and gone into hiding."

"Unless he went into a running panic and has already left town," Jessie suggested, her voice thoughtful. "But when we looked in through the window when we first got here nothing seemed disturbed, the way it would've been if he was getting ready to run."

"If he's gone, then we've already lost his trail," Ki told her. "But I don't think that's the case. And if he's waiting until night to come out here and get whatever he might need, or to destroy papers that would give away any illegal activities he's gotten into, he may not get here for another six or eight hours. If you'd like to go to the hotel and eat supper, Jessie, I can go and have a bite when you get back."

"I'm hungry enough, after missing lunch," she admitted. "But I can't help thinking Perry will show up. There must be papers in his office that he couldn't afford to leave behind, no matter how badly he was spooked."

"Would you like for me to go to the hotel and get us some sandwiches? Or would you rather stretch your legs by walking a little while?"

"If we want to be sure of supper, we'd better eat now. We may not have a chance to, later."

"I'll go and get something, then," Ki volunteered. "And

we'll both feel better when our stomachs have something in them. It's been a long time since breakfast."

"Go ahead," she agreed. As Ki made a last quick survey of the area after standing up, she added, "If there's one thing I learned from Alex—and from you, too, Ki—it's how to be patient."

Ki started along the tracks to the nearest driving lane that crossed them in the checkerboard of stockpens that made up the yards. Jessie watched him for a moment, then turned her attention back to the brokerage office. Her mind was going back through the years to the time when she'd returned hurriedly to the Circle Star from the finishing school she'd been attending in the East after getting word of her father's death.

Alex Starbuck, Jessie's father, had been a self-made industrial and financial tycoon who during a relatively short span of years had created a vast industrial empire that had spanned the United States before his untimely death.

Alex had begun his career as a young man with a small waterfront shop in San Francisco's first booming days, where he'd built up a modest business in oriental imports and curios. He'd bought a single decrepit sailing ship to ply between the Orient and San Francisco to keep his stock replenished, and with the stock as a base had expanded the one shabby vessel into a prosperous merchant shipping line.

It was at this period of Alex's life that Ki had joined him. The son of one of Alex's friends, an American naval officer and his Japanese bride, Ki had been disowned by his mother's aristocratic family because of his mixed blood. When his father was lost at sea, the rootless Ki had decided to become one of the *karateka*, the unarmed warriors who were fighting the tight stranglehold imposed on the common people of Japan by its expansionist elite class.

For several years Ki devoted his time to mastering the arts of unarmed combat, until his skill was unsurpassed. A chance encounter with Alex changed Ki's life. He accepted Alex's offer to join him, and within a few years had become the right-hand man of Jessie's father in business as well as in personal life.

During those years, as his import-export trade grew, Alex had purchased a small decrepit shipyard on San Francisco Bay, and had expanded and modernized it. When the era of iron ships began he'd been one of the first to convert the shipyard to the fabrication of metal-hulled seagoing vessels.

This had led to his acquisition of a steel mill, and Alex's new venture had placed him in a position to prosper even more greatly as American industrial enterprises boomed during the westward expansion in the era of peace which followed the War Between the States. By this time railroads had started crisscrossing the American continent in response to the huge western migration that began after the war years.

Within only a few years the mill had become a major fabricator of railroad cars and rails. Realizing the vast potential of the railroads, Alex had also invested heavily in railroad stocks at the very beginning of the transcontinental transportation boom. As his investments prospered and his industrial holdings grew larger, he'd started acquiring land in many areas of the growing United States, as well as factories to produce the needs of the nation's burgeoning population. He'd needed ready financing for many of his widespread ventures, and this had brought him into brokerage and later into banking.

Young Starbuck's meteoric rise had drawn the attention of the established business community. The day's financial giants had started inviting him in on the ground floor of some of their projects, and by the end of the Civil War Alex was numbered among them as a giant in his own right. However, his new status had also drawn the attention of a sinister European cartel, which saw in the explosion of America's prosperity and power a threat to the supremacy of their declining European empire.

Alex had rejected the cartel's advances when invited to bring his industrial empire into its sphere and become one of its members. More than that, he'd dedicated his personal resources and time to shattering the foreign combine. He'd begun fighting its efforts to take over his homeland in the same ruthless manner it had sponged up the resources of so many European nations.

In spite of his many interests, Alex had not neglected his personal life. He'd married young; but then the wife he adored died giving birth to Jessie. At the time of her death, Alex had just begun to put together the scattered parcels of land that formed the Circle Star ranch.

With a greater land area than some small European nations, the ranch was to have been a haven in which the family he loved could live in peace; but the peace he sought came only in his untimely death in a hail of bullets from killers sent by the European cartel, which could not risk having its secret objectives revealed.

Ki's loyalty to Alex had bonded him to Jessie as strongly as it had to her father. He'd stood by her steadfastly during the troubled years after Jessie had taken up Alex's fight against the cartel. It had taken many fights in many places, but eventually the sinister band had been smashed, its threat to America ended.

In spite of her efforts to move quietly and attract as little attention as possible during the years spent in her fights against the cartel, Jessie had gained the reputation that her father had borne, of being strongly on the side of the small ranchers and farmers and businessmen who were trying to make a place of their own in an increasingly more populous United States.

A short time after the cartel's sinister influence had ended, Jessie realized that the financial and industrial empire she'd inherited was almost unmanageably extensive. Bit by bit, she'd begun trimming away some of the appendages which Alex had acquired or started, such as the brokerage and commodities houses, while still retaining the solid core of its mines and forests and factories and banks.

She did not neglect the other heritage Alex had left her —that of devoting both financial resources and time to helping those who needed a hand in fighting injustice and wrongdoing. While she still looked on the Circle Star as her home and haven, Jessie did not hesitate to act when facing situations such as those she and Ki had now encountered. Though the theft of a few hundred steers would not be a significant loss to the Circle Star, there were other ranchers who would be badly hurt if they lost only a small number from their market herds.

Now, as she thought of the damage that an unscrupulous livestock broker could do to small ranchers whose resources were so much smaller than hers, Jessie became more deeply resolved than ever to follow the leads she and Ki had already uncovered, no matter where they took her. She was still deep in thought when she saw Ki returning, carrying a brown paper sack. He crouched as he entered their hiding place and hunkered down beside her.

"I ran into Arthur Pierce when I was leaving the dining room," he said, "and I asked him if he'd seen anything of Lucas Perry today. He hadn't."

"You didn't tell him what we suspected, did you?" she asked, holding out her hand for the sandwich Ki had taken from the paper sack and was offering her.

"Of course not. But I told Pierce that you're looking for Perry, and he promised to keep an eye out for him."

"I still think he'll show up," Jessie said. "There must be papers in his office, records and letters and ledgers and things like that. Surely there are some that could be used as evidence against him if the law catches up with him, and he'll want to destroy them."

"Of course. It's worth the time we're spending to try to get both Perry and the evidence."

They settled back to their vigil, eating as they watched.

The late afternoon wore on. Though the stockyards hands were still chousing small bunches of cattle from one holding pen to another, the men did not disturb Jessie and Ki, if indeed they were even aware of their presence. Once a locomotive went by on the tracks a few feet from their hiding place, but apparently the engineer and fireman did not see them either.

Dusk was beginning to settle in when Jessie and Ki got the first hint that their long vigil was going to be rewarded. Jessie glimpsed a flicker of motion in the driving lane that ran between the pen where they were hiding and Lucas Perry's office on the other side of the passageway.

"I think Perry's finally gotten here," she said, keeping her voice just above a whisper. "There, across that alley."

Ki looked in the direction she was pointing and nodded. "I see movement, part of a man's body, but the boards of this pen are hiding his face."

"I couldn't see his face either, but if it was one of the men who work here he wouldn't be skulking around the way this one is. He'd be walking right down the middle of the alley to wherever he's heading."

Motionless, Jessie and Ki crouched, poised to move, waiting to get a clear glimpse of the approaching man's face. He reached the door of the office and turned to look around as he fumbled in his pocket, obviously feeling for a key.

"It's Perry, all right," Ki said. "Shall we go after him now, or wait until he gets inside?"

"Now, I think," Jessie replied. "Before he unlocks the door."

She and Ki had formed a team for so many years that when they moved on Lucas Perry there was no need for them to discuss what part each of them was to play. Experience had taught them the best scheme of attack in almost every situation, including the one they now faced: one of them made the attack while the other guarded their quarry's line of escape. As they left their hiding place they separated. Ki started directly toward Perry. He ran erect across the stockpen, not trying to hide or shield himself, depending on the heavy crossbars of the enclosure to blur his body as he raced toward the alleyway.

Jessie ran down the narrow space between the line of stockpens and the railroad spur. Weeds had grown almost chest-high in the small strip of land, and her progress was slower than she'd expected it to be. Finally reaching the spot where she would be able to cut Perry off if he tried to reach the street that led to the center of town, she went across the weedless enclosure swiftly and slid between the thick slats into the alley between two rows of pens.

Once Ki had gotten to the alleyway he stopped momentarily to be sure that Perry had not noticed him. Ducking between the slats, he stepped into the alley and dropped flat. Now he moved *ninja*-style, dropping on all fours, his torso parallel to the ground as he crossed the alley and reached the concealment of the fence that formed the pens between him and Perry.

Perry had gone into his office now. Though the gathering dusk was quickly shadowing into night and the interior

68

of Perry's office must have been almost dark, the swindler did not light a lamp. Before Ki had reached the corner of the cattle-alley that ran between the pens, Lucas came out of his office. His arms were loaded with papers which he carried a step or two away from the office shack and let slide to the ground.

A match flared and the swindling broker touched its flame to the papers he'd let fall. A small line of fire ran along the edges of the piled papers as they started burning. Perry stood watching them as more and more of the documents caught fire. It was as though the spreading flickers fascinated him. He did not turn to look around, but stood staring at the crawling lines of the spreading flames.

Ki decided to abandon his cautious approach; he saw that the cattle-broker was so engrossed in watching the small bonfire he'd started that it was unlikely he'd look around. He stood erect, getting his balance for the final quick run he'd now planned to make. But before he could begin his spurt Perry turned away from the fast-spreading fire and went back into the office. Ki stopped short. The corner of the fence around the pen that hid him from Lucas blocked his view, and he was too wise in the ways of invisible approach to show himself again until his quarry had no chance to see him.

Jessie had run along the railroad track along the back ends of three or four of the small stockpens until she reached the wider alleyway that ran at a right angle between the pens to the hotel. Once she saw her objective in the gathering gloom she left the railroad tracks and crossed through the stockpens until she got to the main passage leading to the hotel and the streets of Fort Worth which lay beyond it. The swift moves that she and Ki made had taken only a few minutes.

As Jessie looked back to find Ki, she saw the flicker of

flame from the match Perry was just striking to set fire to the papers he'd taken out of the brokerage office. To anyone else, Ki would have been invisible in his dark blue cotton blouse and trousers, crouching beside the corner of the pens in front of the brokerage office, but Jessie could see his head and shoulders outlined as the fire Perry had just lighted flared into life. She stopped and waited, to be ready when Ki made his final dash and closed in on their quarry.

She saw Perry return to the office, and she noticed that Ki was visible now, his crouched form a black, shapeless blob outlined by the red, dancing glow as the intensity of the flames increased. Perry came out of the office, his arms again piled with papers to toss on the fire he'd started. As he dumped the documents on the blaze, Ki moved.

Two or three long strides brought him within striking distance of his quarry. Ki now abandoned his *ninja* approach, and left the cover of the shadowing stockpen fence and dashed toward the swindler. He was not prepared for the half-liquid puddle of still-fresh steer manure that his feet hit before he'd covered half the distance between him and Perry. In the darkness before the swindler had lighted his fire, and then with the flames bursting into life and half-blinding him momentarily, Ki's normally swift advance was slowed as he twisted to keep on his feet.

Perry turned away from the fire and saw Ki as a black shadow in the wide alley between the pens and the brokerage office. The sight jarred Perry's already tense nerves. He turned and began running in the instant or two before Ki could recover his balance.

As he ran, Perry slid a heavy revolver from a crossdraw holster. Though Ki was still trying to find solid footing in the slippery puddle, his razor-keen reactions had not deserted him. He flicked a *shuriken* from the vest pocket in which he carried the throwing-blades.

Perry was turning to run when Ki spun the *shuriken*. A flash of silvery metal marked its course as the razor-keen blade arced through the air and sliced into Perry's shoulder. His gun hand sagged, and the shot he'd intended for Ki raised a puff of dust in the stockpen beyond him.

Ki's feet finally gritted on solid ground, and he leaped clear of the manure puddle, but the delay of those few floundering moments had disrupted his scheme of attack. By the time he'd freed himself, Perry had dashed across the passageway between the stockpens and ducked below the bottom rail into the pen, where the fence and the darkness hid him from even Ki's keen eyes.

Jessie had watched the fiasco that spoiled Ki's attack, but with Ki between her and Perry she'd been unwilling to shoot at the swindling broker because Ki's form was almost directly in line with Perry's swiveling figure. She started running across the wide alleyway at an angle that would give her a clear shot at Perry, but before she was able to trigger off a round the fleeing criminal had ducked into the stockpen and vanished in the darkness of the enclosure.

By this time Ki was out of the little slippery morass that had spoiled his plan of attack, but Perry was no longer visible. Ki started toward the stockpen into which the swindling broker had vanished just as Jessie came up to him.

"Which way did he go?" she asked.

"I couldn't tell," Ki answered.

"He's probably running along the railroad track toward town," she said. "You start down the alley. I'll go through the pen and try to catch up with him. He hasn't had time to get too far away."

"What about the fire?"

71

"It'll burn itself out quickly; it's only paper. Getting Lucas Perry's more important."

With a quick nod, Ki started running down the alley. Jessie ducked between the fence rails and crossed the pen. She ducked between the slats onto the railroad track just as a locomotive rounded the slight curve in the tracks and silhouetted Perry's running form.

His body outlined in black against the glare of the locomotive's headlight turned the fleeing swindler into a perfect target, and Jessie brought up her Colt.

Perry had seen the opportunity that the oncoming train offered as a means of quick escape. He'd realized at once that if he could put the train between himself and Jessie and Ki, he stood a good chance of getting away in the darkness that shrouded the maze of stockpens on the other side of the tracks, and as Jessie was raising her Colt the fugitive was turning to leap across the tracks.

As Jessie swung her Colt to get Lucas in her sights, the fleeing swindler leaped. His haste to jump was his undoing. The loose gravel of the roadbed grated under the soles of Lucas's boots as he launched his leap. He fell short, directly in front of the locomotive. The shriek of pain which he loosed as the engine's wheels rumbled across his prone body was lost in the belated blast of the engine's whistle. A metallic shriek filled the evening air as the engineer threw on the brakes, but it was too late.

★

Chapter 7

Ki caught up with Jessie as she stood beside the track. He said, "I saw what happened. We'd better talk to the engineer and tell him what Perry was doing when the train hit him."

"And I suppose the authorities will have to be notified, too," Jessie added. "But Arthur Pierce has enough influence to keep us from having to spend a lot of time with them."

"We'd better go back to the hotel and tell him what's going on, and how it all happened," Ki suggested.

"We will, as soon as we've looked through Perry's office. He may have burned everything important, but there may be something he's overlooked that will prove he and his company in Chicago were swindlers."

"He had plenty of time to destroy anything that might've helped us," Ki pointed out.

"I don't expect to find much, Ki, but it'd be helpful if we find something that will show how deeply his bosses in the main office of that Chicago brokerage house are involved in the thefts."

Ki nodded. "Everything indicates they're in up to the hilt. But you go ahead and start looking, Jessie. I'll talk to the trainmen and tell them we'll see Pierce later, in his office."

Jessie hurried to the dead cattle broker's office. She lit the lamp on the wall, then turned in the doorway, surveying a scene of total disarray. The drawers of the crooked broker's big rolltop desk were open and empty, so were the three oak filling cabinets. Scraps of torn or crumpled letters, ledger sheets, telegraph flimsies and other papers strewed the floor. She was still standing inside the door, looking for a place to start, when Ki joined her.

"It looks hopeless, doesn't it?" she asked him.

"I think it is hopeless, Jessie. Perry knew what he had to do, and he made quick work of it. I'm sure there's nothing left in here that would help us."

"Then we'll go to Chicago, Ki," she said. "I think I can persuade Arthur Pierce to delay notifying Perry's bosses of his death until we have time to get there."

"And if they find out anyhow?"

"It's a risk we'll take," she replied decisively. "I'm not just thinking of the money he stole from the Circle Star, Ki. We're not the only ones Perry swindled. He must've been cheating other ranchers, too, and a lot of them aren't in as good shape as we are. The only way we can find out and stop that crooked brokerage outfit once and for all is to get to their headquarters before the real brains of the gang learn what's happened."

"Then we'd better go back to the hotel and see about train schedules," Ki said.

"We don't have time to waste," she told him. "I'll get Arthur to arrange for a special train, a locomotive and one sleeping-car. We won't have any trouble getting a clear track. We can be in Chicago day after tomorrow."

"It's odd, Ki, but in Chicago I always feel like I'm a stranger," Jessie commented as the hack that was taking them from the depot slowed to round the corner into State Street. Ahead, on the corner of Monroe, the imposing bulk of the Palmer House came into view. She went on, "Even though we've been here several times, things seem to change faster than they do in other cities. Only the Palmer House looks familiar to me."

"Don't you suppose the big fire had something to do with the way you feel about the city changing?"

"It may have." She nodded. "The first time I was here was when Alex was taking me East to Miss Booth's Academy, and that was before the fire. Just as you and I are doing now, we took a hack to the Palmer House. Father and Colonel Palmer were good friends, you remember."

"Yes, I remember the colonel quite well."

"Then when I came back, only about two or three years later, everything was different. There were still traces of the fire everywhere, the colonel was just rebuilding the Palmer House, and—well, everything was different. And I guess it always will seem different to me." She looked out of the carriage as the hackman wheeled it into the hotel's wide porte-cochere. Then she went on, "But I'll give the colonel a lot of credit. The new Palmer House looks just like the first one did."

A portly doorman wearing an ankle-length coat and a gray stovepipe hat opened the carriage door almost before the vehicle came to a stop. "Welcome to the Palmer House," he said. "Your bellman is on his way now to take care of your luggage and show you to your rooms."

75

Almost before the man finished speaking, the bellman came out the high bronze doors. He made a bobbing half-bow to Jessie and Ki as he told them, "If you've reserved your accomodations, you can register later if you prefer to, and I can show you to your rooms at once, if that's your pleasure."

"I wired for reservations before we left Texas," Jessie told him. "My name is Jessica Starbuck."

"Miss Starbuck, of course," the bellman nodded. "We were told to expect you. I hope you had a pleasant trip?"

"Very satisfactory and very fast," Jessie said. "And we'd like to go to our suite immediately, though I'd better stop at the desk to see if I have a message I'm expecting."

Jessie and Ki followed the bellman through a wide passageway, and as they made their way along it they got quick glimpses of the high-ceilinged billiard parlor and the marble-tiled barber-shop with its silver dollars embedded in the corner of each tile. They entered the soaring lobby, a place of Persian rugs and luxurious custom-crafted lounges and armchairs, and stopped at the mahogany counter of the registration desk. Through some alchemy of hotelmanship which Jessie neither understood nor questioned, the room clerk addressed her by name, although to her knowledge he had never seen her before.

"Welcome to the Palmer House, Miss Starbuck," he said. "Colonel Palmer has asked me to give you his regards and to tell you that he would like to have you join him as his guest for dinner, if you find it convenient."

"That's very thoughtful of him," Jessie replied. "I'll be glad to see the colonel again."

"Then he will call for you at eight o'clock," the man went on. "Your suite is ready. And if you care to register now—"

Jessie nodded and signed her name and Ki's on the opened page of the massive leatherbound volume the clerk pushed toward her. While she was signing her name and adding Ki's, the man turned to the pigeonholed wall behind the counter and took out an envelope, which he handed to her as she laid down the pen.

"This was delivered by hand earlier today," he said. "We were asked to notify the gentleman whose name is on the envelope when you arrived. Is that your pleasure?"

Without glancing at the engraved inscription on the envelope, Jessie nodded. "Please do. And have him shown up at once when he gets here."

"I'll send a messenger immediately," the clerk promised. "And I hope that your stay with us will be a pleasant one."

Jessie acknowledged the man's words with a silent nod, and as she and Ki turned to follow the bellman to the elevator, Ki said in a half-whisper, "I don't know how they know your name, either, Jessie. I remember Alex asking Colonel Palmer once how his people managed that little trick, but the colonel only looked wise and winked and shook his head."

"I think the colonel enjoys having his little secrets." She smiled. "Perhaps we can find out at dinner this evening."

After the bellman had gone through the routine of placing their luggage on racks in the bedrooms and adjusting the windows and blinds and gone on his way, Jessie opened the envelope the clerk had given her. After she'd read the brief note it contained she told Ki, "Jason Maxwell will be getting here soon. And if anybody can give us the real truth about that Blossom and Bond brokerage house, it's Jason."

"Yes, Alex always said that nobody in Chicago could keep a secret as long as Mr. Maxwell had his law firm here. And he also said that even if he didn't always follow Mr. Maxwell's advice, his firm wasn't just the best in Chicago, but the best in the entire country."

"I don't know about you," Jessie went on, "but I'm going to bathe and change clothes before he gets here. I feel like I'm a solid mass of cinders after that trip from Fort Worth."

"Go ahead, then. I'll wait for my bath until you're through, in case Mr. Maxwell shows up before you finish."

"I'm sorry that all my news is going to be bad, Jessie," Jason Maxwell said after he and Jessie and Ki had exchanged greetings. "But Blossom and Bond simply doesn't exist any longer."

"You mean they've closed?" She frowned.

"They just shut down tight and vanished," Maxwell replied. "As soon as I got your telegram from Fort Worth, I sent one of those bright young men I'm training over to their office. I told him to keep asking questions until he got some answers. The door of their office was locked, and he asked the superintendent of the building to open it for him. The superintendent was as surprised as my man had been to find the door locked and nobody at work inside the office."

"But did he let your man in?" Jessie asked.

"No, but don't worry about that. We're getting a court order to open the office. It should be issued today. Then we can see what kind of records they left."

"I can't believe that a business as big as Blossom and Bond must have been could just close down overnight and everybody connected with it disappear." Jessie frowned.

"Oh, things of that sort do happen," the attorney said. "And since you wired me, I've started checking up on Blossom and Bond. In fact, there are three attorneys from my office working right now to trace the men behind the firm."

"Have you found out anything that will help us?"

"Nothing except that there isn't anyone named Blossom or Bond connected with it anymore. They simply sold out to a man named Fredrick Wasson, who seems to've been a confidence artist in Saint Louis before moving here. Of course, he'd have had very good reason not to change the firm's name; I've found that he has a record at bunco schemes. He's also good at hiding his loot. I'm afraid you'll never recover a penny of the cattle losses you've suffered on your ranch."

"I'm not worried about what the Circle Star's lost, Jason. It's the small ranchers who were swindled that need all the help they can to get back the money their steers would've brought in."

"Jessie, the long and the short of it is that until my men or the police run down Wasson or some of his men, there's not much anybody can do." Maxwell shrugged and shook his head. "My men will do their best, though."

"Do you really think there'll be any money left to get back, by the time you find them?" Ki asked.

Maxwell shook his head. "No. Swindlers and other crooks spend money faster than they can steal it, Ki. But there'll be a certain amount of satisfaction in seeing them go to jail." He turned to Jessie and asked, "I'm assuming that's what you had in mind, as well as recovering anything that can be salvaged?"

Jessie nodded. "I'll cover your fees, Jason."

"There won't be any. Attorneys are supposed to do a certain amount of work for the public good. This will be part of it. And now that we've settled the details, are you and Ki going to have dinner with me this evening?"

"Oh, I'm sorry, but we've already accepted an invitation from Colonel Palmer," Jessie said.

"Now, that's a shame, but I won't try to deprive the colonel of your company. However, since I got your telegram, I've been thinking of you in connection with another client of mine. He's started a cattle operation that you might be interested in looking at."

"Not another ranch!" Jessie exclaimed. "I don't want anything except the Circle Star."

"This isn't ranching as we usually think of it," Maxwell told her. "In a way, it's an extension of ranching, but it goes quite a bit further."

"In what way?"

"Now, let me keep asking the questions for a minute or two, Jessie. First of all, how much difference is there between the amount of money you get for a steer and the amount a butcher pays for the beef he sells across the counter?"

"Quite a bit, of course." Jessie frowned. "But since we don't buy meat for the ranch, I've never stopped to figure it out. Why?"

"Whys can come later," Maxwell replied. "But since you don't know the answer to my question, I'll answer it for you. If you sell a steer on the hoof for—well, say three hundred dollars—the broker's going to sell it to the slaughterhouse for three hundred and thirty, and the slaughterhouse is going to sell the skinned and dressed carcass to a butcher for three-fifty or three-seventy-five, and the butcher's going to add ten or twelve percent of what he's paid to the meat he sells across the counter of his shop. Does that sound about right?"

"I can't argue about your figures, because I don't know, Jason," Jessie told him. "But I'm sure they must be right, or you wouldn't be using them."

"And if you could ship your cattle to market as sides of beef, you could sell to the butcher at the slaughterhouse price, couldn't you?" Maxwell went on.

"I suppose so." Jessie nodded after a moment's thought.

"Then you'd be getting anywhere from fifty to seventy-five dollars a head more for every steer you sell," Maxwell went on, shaking a finger for emphasis in courtroom fashion. "And I don't have to tell you how much more the Circle Star would be earning every year."

"No, I've been adding it up myself while you were talking." Jessie smiled. "But the Circle Star's a ranch, Jason. It's not a slaughterhouse, and I don't have any intention of turning it into one."

"In that case, I don't suppose you'd be interested in meeting the man I mentioned a moment ago, the one who's being very successful right this minute in combining cattle ranching with a slaughterhouse," the lawyer went on.

"Are you telling me that someone's actually doing what you've been pretending to suggest?"

"That's what I've been leading up to."

Jessie was silent for a moment. Then she said thoughtfully, "I've known you since I was a little girl, Jason, and you've never given me any bad advice or suggestions. If you think I ought to meet this friend—or client, I suppose—of yours, I'm certainly not going to refuse. But I'd like to know a little more about him first."

"He's a French nobleman, Jessie. The Marquis de Mores. He came to the States several years ago with his wife, who's an American girl, by the way."

Ki had been listening to the conversation between Jessie and the lawyer. Now he asked, "Where is this combination ranch and slaughterhouse, Mr. Maxwell?"

"West, in the Dakota Territory. De Mores has actually built a pretty sizable town around several sections of land he bought. He's named it Medora, after his wife. It's just occurred to me that you may have met her, Jessie. Her father's Von Hoffman, the New York banker."

Jessie shook her head. "No. But it isn't important."

"Well," Maxwell continued, "de Mores has put up a house—really a French-style castle, or 'chateau,' as he calls it. And he seems to be doing well."

"Is he in Chicago now?" Jessie asked.

Maxwell nodded. "To look at these new ice-making machines. I understand he's had some problems with meat spoiling in the boxcars while it's being shipped."

"Well, if your invitation to dinner still stands, I'd be very interested in meeting him," she said. "Particularly since it seems we're going to be staying here several days."

"Good. Let's say tomorrow, here at the Palmer House," Maxwell suggested. "Ki, you know that you're included in my invitation, of course. And by then I'll try to have some real information about Wasson and the brokerage house, Jessie."

"You paint a fascinating picture of your new venture and its possibilities, Marquis," Jessie said as the French nobleman fell silent. "When Jason told me about it, I had no idea that you were operating on such a large scale."

"You must really see my plant yourself to understand how efficient it is, Mademoiselle Starbuck," de Mores went on. "I've only told you a small portion of the story."

During the first moments after Jason Maxwell had introduced Jessie and Ki to de Mores in the Palmer House lobby, the Frenchman had been relatively silent. De Mores was a tall man, thin to the point of angularity. He was much younger than Jessie had anticipated; she guessed him now to be in his late twenties or early thirties, though at first glance his angular features had seemed to add several years to his age.

If Jessie had been unkind, she'd have described de Mores as being hatchet-faced. His nose was overlong for his narrow cheekbones and came to a sharp point which was made to seem even sharper by the stiffly waxed moustache that jutted out like a pair of horizontal black icicles on either side of his sunken cheeks. The contours of his moustache were repeated in the short conical beard which concealed his chin and drew to a sharp point a couple of inches below it. His cheeks were shaved clean and heavily powdered, his lips a bit over-full. His dark eyes flashed magnetically as he spoke, and the flow of his language was just a bit overwhelming, especially since he gestured almost incessantly with long, thin hands to emphasize his words.

"Yes," he repeated, "you really must see my plant before you can form a true judgment. Medora and I would be honored if you chose to visit us while you are so close to our chateau."

"Excuse me," Ki said when the Frenchman paused. "But you speak of your town as though it were a person."

"But Medora *is* a person!" the Marquis exclaimed. "I was referring to my wife when I spoke. You must understand, Ki, that when I decided to begin my venture here, I did not want to go to a place where there would be distractions. I decided that a new community must be the solution, especially here in America, where there is so much land being wasted. There were other considerations, to be sure, but solitude and the great open prairie of your country..." He paused and smiled, his white teeth flashing. Then he added, "Your country and mine, Ki, as well as that of the native Indians and so many from crowded Europe who have come here to make new homes. So I sought an unsettled place to begin a town as well as an enterprise, and the Dakota Territory was my solution. And what better name could I find? I gave my town the name of my dear wife to honor her."

"You know, Jessie, what the marquis is talking about may just be something that you'll see much more of in the future," Jason Maxwell said thoughtfully. "A young fellow named Andrew Carnegie came into my office the other day. He wanted some help in negotiating a deal he's trying to make to buy a small steelyard. He's very bright, and we got to talking. He has the idea that what he called industrial integration is something we'll see a lot of in the future."

"My idea exactly!" de Mores exclaimed. "One large plant or factory to take the steers and of them make sides of beef for delivery to the markets! A beef factory, if you please! That is what I am doing now. I must meet this young man the next time I am in Chicago, Jason!"

The lawyer nodded. "I'll see if I can arrange it." Then, turning back to Jessie, he went on, "It doesn't really make much sense for you to ship live steers from Texas to Fort Worth, where they're sorted and shipped on to Chicago or Saint Louis to be slaughtered and turned into sides of beef that're shipped back to butcher shops in Texas to be sold to housewives."

"I see you've finally come around to my way of thinking, Jason." The Marquis smiled, then turned to Jessie and went on, "If you will only accept my invitation to visit me at Medora, you can see in a very short time what I am trying to explain."

Jessie glanced across the table at Ki, who gave an almost imperceptible shrug. She looked at Jason Maxwell and the marquis, and saw that both of them were waiting for her reply.

"All right," she said slowly. "I'll accept your thoughtful invitation, Marquis. Ki and I will go back to Medora with you and take a look at your beef factory."

Chapter 8

"Why, when the marquis was describing his plant to us, I didn't really grasp how big it is, if that big chimney we see ahead is any indication of its size," Jessie commented.

She and Ki had gotten their first indication that they were nearing the end of their long trip from Chicago a full half-hour earlier, when above the flattened horizon of the broken, ridge-clumped terrain the tip of a cylindrical smokestack first became visible from the windows of the Great Northern passenger coach.

Since sighting the stack's tip they'd watched it push higher and higher into the sky, and had begun to catch occasional glimpses of the glint of running water beyond it, a river that wound through the rough broken country west of the huge chimney. The sun had set before they could make out the base of the stack and the long low lines of the massive brick building that stood at its base, but the cloudless sky still glowed brightly, not yet darkened by the approaching dusk.

As the train drew steadily closer there was still enough after-sunset light for them to make out the forty or fifty small, scattered houses and about the same number of conical Indian tipis that stretched in huddled clumps around the huge brick structure. Now they could also see that the glints of water which had from time to time been reflecting the sun's rays came from a small stream that wound through the broken terrain just beyond the settlement.

"I couldn't belive it at first, either," Ki admitted. "When we first saw that tall chimney I thought for a moment that it was a natural rock formation. I still can't quite convince myself that it's actually as big as it looks now."

They fell silent, gazing through the windows of the slowing train's passenger coach at the huge red-brick structure which was just coming into full view. The gentle curve ended as the tracks straightened, approaching the river, but they were still able to see what could only be the Marquis de Mores's beef plant.

Now that they could see both chimney and building clearly, they found that the plant building was in its own way almost as imposing as its smokestack. The red brick structure seemed to be a mile long. It extended on both sides beyond the scattering of small houses and tipis that constituted the town. There seemed to be neither rhyme nor reason for their location; tipis and frame houses intermingled at random.

On the tumble-heaped, striated prairie beyond the town, a mile or so past the west bank of the river, Jessie now saw the outline of a house. It stood on a low hillock that was the only prominent rise visible against the horizon. As the train drew closer she corrected her first impression, for the house was a mansion which even at this distance was no less impressive than the beef factory and its smoke-stack.

"It's a chateau!" Ki exclaimed when he turned his eyes to follow Jessie's after her exclamation of surprise. "Just like one that you'd find in France. When Alex took me with him on some of his trips to Europe, I saw a lot of them in France, mostly along the river valleys."

Jessie nodded abstractedly. She was still studying the big, blocky building on the hill. The distance was a bit too great for her to make out details, but through the clear prairie air she could tell that the chateau was constructed of pale quarrystone, was three stories tall, and had the form of an almost square block broken by many wide windows. It stood alone on its hillock, perhaps a mile or more from the town itself. In its own fashion, but equally as effectively as did the factory, the chateau dominated its treeless surroundings just as the plant and its towering chimney dominated the small town.

"You know, Ki, the marquis seems to be determined to turn this part of the country into something resembling his native land," Jessie commented.

"That same idea occurred to me, too," Ki replied. "But if he is, I'd say he's facing an impossible job. Even if there were trees and shrubs and perhaps a vineyard or two in sight, I'd know we were in the Dakota Territory instead of France."

Jessie nodded abstractedly. She'd kept her eyes on the house while Ki was talking, and she said now, "It looks to me like we're going to have a reception committee waiting for us."

Ki's gaze followed Jessie's gesturing hand. He saw four riders, two of them leading horses, starting from the chateau down the long barren slope that led to the town. As the quartet moved away from the imposing building a buckboard came into sight from behind it and followed them.

"It looks as though we'll be well escorted to the marquis's home," Ki told her, adding, "I'm sure that's it, and from the way it looks at a distance we'll be very comfortable while we're staying in Medora. Which reminds me, we haven't talked about how long we're going to be here."

"I haven't given that a great deal of thought myself, Ki. We don't have any real reason to hurry back. Since we haven't been away from the Circle Star for quite a while, I had an idea that after so much hurrying around it might do us good to count this as a sort of vacation. We could go back by way of Denver and stop off there for a few days before heading home."

Ki nodded. "I'd enjoy that. And from what Jason Maxwell said before we left Chicago, there's not going to be anything new on that situation for quite a while, so we can take our time about getting back."

"If it hadn't been for Jason's urging me to look at what the marquis is doing, we wouldn't be here at all. And I don't think I've mentioned it before, but Jason told me confidentially that the marquis is getting a bit worried about investing so heavily in this beef operation."

"I thought he was rich enough to do just about anything he wanted to, regardless of cost."

"From what Jason told me, the marquis is worrying about his resources in Europe, especially in France. No one except Europeans is concerned about it, but the French are on the verge of having to fight another war in North Africa right now."

Ki nodded. "Which could mean that the marquis might lose a great deal of money, I suppose?"

"Something like that. Jason didn't give me a lot of details about the situation. But he hinted that the marquis might be looking for a partner, and half-suggested that I give some thought to investing in this cattle venture here."

"How do you feel about it?"

"Just as I've felt about similar situations before. I keep asking myself what Alex would've done, and when I'm sure I've worked out the answer I do what seems best."

"Then there's not much chance that you'll do the wrong thing, Jessie," Ki said encouragingly.

"It's always worked out before," she replied. "Anyhow, I'll see what the marquis is doing here and make up my mind later. And judging by what we're looking at now from the train, it's not going take long for him to show us everything there is to see."

Even before Jessie had finished speaking, the conductor came into the coach. "This is your stop, Miss Starbuck," he said. "We don't call stations like this one out here in the Dakota Territory, because for a long time some of the Easterners that were ticketed to get off at places like it tried to back out at the last minute when they saw what these whistle-stops looked like."

Jessie smiled. "That won't be a problem with us, because at home, down in Texas, we get off at a whistle-stop smaller than this one."

Ki had already taken their valises off the luggage rack. He carried them down the coach aisle, following Jessie and the conductor to the front of the car as the train came to a stop with a screeching of brake shoes on steel wheels. The car in which they'd been seated had stopped behind the huge brick building, and its high walls hid the town from them.

Just as they alighted the horsemen they'd seen leaving the chateau appeared around the corner of the long brick building. Astride a coal-black stallion, the Marquis de Mores had now taken the position of leader. His entourage formed a short parade behind him, the buckboard bringing up in the rear. He reined up in front of Jessie and Ki and bowed from the waist.

"Welcome to Medora, Miss Starbuck," he said. "And you, too, of course, Ki. I'm sure that after such a long journey you will wish to go directly to my chateau to rest and refresh yourselves, instead of riding through the town and observing it. That we can do later."

"Whatever you've arranged or have in mind will be perfectly satisfactory with Ki and me," Jessie replied.

"There is, of course, no social life here as yet," de Mores said with a shrug. He swept his arm in a gesture that encompassed the straggling community and added, "That day will arrive, as my town grows into a city. But we shall go now to the chateau. Would you prefer to ride in the buckboard, or on one of the horses? You will see that I've provided one with a sidesaddle, as I assumed you would not be wearing the proper skirt to ride astride."

"I'd prefer the horse, Marquis," Jessie told him. "And I'll manage with the sidesaddle, thank you."

"We'll start at once, then," de Mores said. "One of my men will see that your luggage is placed in the wagon."

Jessie swung lithely into the sidesaddle, ignoring the man from de Mores's entourage who dismounted and started toward her to help her mount. The skirt she was wearing was ankle-length and fairly full, but did not have the billowing yards of extra material called for by the day's fashion to cover her feet in the twin stirrups after she'd mounted. The marquis's attendants stared in an effort to get a glimpse of her legs, and turned away in disappointment when they saw the calf-high boots that she'd chosen for the trip.

Ki had already settled into the saddle of the second horse. De Mores glanced around, making sure his small retinue was ready, then reined up beside Jessie.

"We will ride directly for my chateau," he said to Jessie. "The day grows late, and there will be time later for you to inspect the plant and the town I have begun to create."

"I was surprised at the size of both," Jessie told him as she toed her horse into motion to ride beside the marquis. "And I was also quite surprised to see so many tipis; there are almost as many of them as there are houses. You must hire quite a few Indian workers in your plant."

He nodded. "All but a dozen or so are Sioux; their tribes are greater in number than others in this part of the Dakota Territory. But I find them to be good workers, and they are skilled from childhood at butchering."

Ki, riding beside Jessie and the Frenchman, asked their host, "How many men do you have working?"

"Almost two hundred. I'm sure that within a few years I will need to employ an even larger number as my method of providing beef becomes accepted by more and more meat dealers. But these are things we can discuss later. We must leave now if we are to reach the chateau before darkness falls."

A warning whistle sounded from the locomotive as it whuffed into motion, and the train began pulling away. It passed them quickly, and as the last car cleared the tracks the marquis led his small group toward the skeletonlike railroad bridge that spanned the stream. Jessie and Ki got only a brief glimpse of the oddly-assorted town as they rode, for the marquis set a brisk pace in leading them to the river.

They reached the stream below the railroad bridge. It ran glass-clear, and even in the fast-fading light Jessie could see that the bottom was mostly dark-hued sand. The water was shallow and at its deepest rose little higher than the horse's fetlocks when they splashed across. The lightly laden buckboard lurched a bit on the uneven riverbed, but had no trouble keeping pace with the horsemen at the easy pace set by de Mores.

Ahead of them the sudden onset of the fast-falling prairie night had now turned the chateau into a bulky black outline against the thin bright strip at the distant horizon. Night's descent seemed to magnify the size of the building and make it even more imposing than it had looked earlier. The darkening sky created the illusion that the house was increasing in size as they drew close to the low rise on which it stood. The last line of twilight was showing behind the building, and lights now glowed in several of its windows.

As the marquis led the way to the arched portico that broke the severely plain face of the bulky, square-cut mansion the double doors opened and two women stepped out. Yellow candlelight from the wide doorway formed a small strip in front of the building and showed the shadowed figures of two men as they ran around the corner of the house.

While the women were advancing to the edge of the narrow porch, the riders reined in. One of the men who'd appeared so suddenly and unexpectedly ran to Jessie's horse and grabbed its bridle. The other performed the same service for the marquis.

De Mores made no effort to dismount, but waited until the man running toward him had grasped his stirrup. Only then did the marquis rise and leave his saddle. The pair of grooms who'd accompanied the party had slid from their saddles at once and were hurrying up to assist Jessie, but she was already swinging off her horse.

Ki had been the first to dismount. He got his feet on the ground and stood watching the marquis's retainers as they scurried around. He stepped up to Jessie and whispered,

"We're obviously not accustomed to associating with nobility, Jessie. I see now that we should've waited for the servants to help us dismount."

"As long as I can move, I'm going to mount and dismount without anybody's assistance, Ki," she whispered back. "But I was as confused as you were by the attention we're being given."

During the brief exchange between Jessie and Ki, de Mores was hurrying up to them. "My men were very lax, Miss Starbuck. I must beg your forgiveness for their inattention."

"Don't worry about it," Jessie said. "But we're a bit less formal on the Circle Star, and we're not used to this kind of hospitality."

"It will not happen again, I assure you," de Mores said. He crooked his elbow as he spoke. "Now, if you will honor me by allowing me to escort you into my chateau, I will present you to the marquise."

Concealing her amusement at the overly formal reception that was apparently routine at the chateau, Jessie rested her hand on de Mores's arm and mounted the steps to the narrow porch. Light streaming through the open double doors turned the two waiting women into silhouettes. The faces of the Marquise de Mores and her companion were in deep shadow, and the only detail of her hostess's appearance that was clear to Jessie's eyes was the cascade of deep red hair that spread across her shoulders.

His voice gravely formal, de Mores said, "My dear, allow me to present to you Miss Jessica Starbuck. Miss Starbuck, the Marquise de Mores."

"Welcome, Miss Starbuck," the marquise said. "My husband has mentioned you often since his return from Chicago. I'm very pleased that you could find time to visit us."

To Jessie's surprise, her hostess spoke without a trace of a foreign accent; her voice held the soft slurring rhythm of the American south. She replied, "Thank you, Marquise. I'm sure we'll enjoy our stay."

As she took the hand the marquise extended, Jessie realized that de Mores had no intention of introducing Ki. She turned to him and went on, "And this is my invaluable assistant, Marquise. His name is Ki."

If the marquise was surprised by Jessie's introduction, she showed no sign of it. She inclined her head as she turned to Ki and said, "We are happy that you have come with Miss Starbuck, Ki. Welcome to our home."

Ki bowed. "Thank you, Marquise. I am pleased to be here."

De Mores broke into the conversation. "Train schedules are so uncertain here that we were not sure exactly when you would arrive, Miss Starbuck. I asked Medora to defer your welcoming dinner until tomorrow evening, when we will offer you a suitable repast."

When the nobleman paused, the marquise took up the thread of his remark and added, "This evening, you will be served a light supper in your rooms. I hope this pleases you?"

"Of course," Jessie replied. "And I'm sure Ki will agree with me. It's been quite a long trip, and we'll both appreciate the chance to feel solid floors under our feet instead of the jolting and swaying of a railway coach."

"Then Bliss will show you to your rooms, Miss Starbuck," the marquise went on, gesturing toward the maidservant who'd stepped to the side of the group while they talked. "She will stay to help you unpack, if you wish, and—"

"Please, Marquise!" Jessie broke in. "I appreciate your thoughtfulness, but I'm used to packing and unpacking without any help. If she'll just show me where my room is, I won't deprive you of her services."

"As you wish." The marquise nodded, then went on, "I have arranged a small suite upstairs for you and Monsieur Ki, a drawing room with adjoining bedchambers. You will be served breakfast there as well, of course. Then, later in the morning, I'm sure my husband will want to escort you into town to observe the factory of which we are both so proud."

"Thank you, my dear," de Mores said, nodding to his wife. Turning to Jessie, he added, "If you find yourself sufficiently rested, we will go in mid-morning to look at my plant."

"That'll be fine, Marquis," Jessie replied. "After the glimpse we got of it from the train, I'm quite interested in seeing it."

"I'll confess that I didn't expect to find anything like this in the Dakota Territory," Jessie told Ki as they sat at the table after supper.

They'd talked little while they ate. Their dinner had been brought up on large trays carried by a liveried man-servant: thin slices of roast venison haunch served with a wine sauce, young green peas almost as small as birdshot, tender stalks of asparagus, crusty rolls, and sugar-crusted macaroons with strong black coffee kept warm by a spirit lamp.

"From what we've seen, I'd say the marquis is still a very rich man, in spite of what Jason Maxwell said," Ki replied. "At least his standard of living matches his title. All that his chateau lacks is the patina of age that's so apparent in the ones I saw when I was in Europe with Alex."

"That's something that will never be missed here in the

Dakota Territory." Jessie smiled. "And if his factory is anything like his household, he should be doing very well with his beef-selling operation. Still, it's expensive to keep up this style of living in a place like this. His house and that huge plant certainly show that he must've spent a great deal of money."

"Do I get a hint that you're thinking of investing in his plant, then?"

"No. At least, not until I've gone through it and looked at some of his recent operating statements," Jessie answered. A thoughtful frown growing on her face, she added, "But what he's doing does make a lot of sense, Ki. Just think about what that crooked broker in Fort Worth has cost the Circle Star."

Ki nodded. "Yes. But losses like that haven't been common, and it's not likely that the same thing will happen again."

"I certainly don't intend to let something of that sort happen again!" Jessie exclaimed. Then, with her thoughtful frown reappearing, she went on, "And think about the time we spend driving our market herds to the railroad and the cost of shipping them. If we had a plant on the Circle Star like the one we got a glimpse of in Medora today, we'd be saving a great deal of money."

"I can't argue with you about that," Ki agreed. "I suppose the most important thing I learned from your father is that new innovations have to be considered in any business."

"Yes, he was—" Jessie broke off as a sharp but distant crackling reached their ears.

They listened for a moment in silence as the small explosive noises grew in intensity.

"That's gunfire, Ki!" Jessie exclaimed.

"Yes."

96

Ki was already on his feet. Jessie jumped from her chair and followed him to the draperies that hung from the ceiling at one side of the room. When they pulled the heavy silk fabric aside, through the blackness of the prairie night they could see small red spurts of flame in the distance.

"It's gunfire, all right," Ki went on. "Somebody is attacking Medora!"

★

Chapter 9

Even before Ki had spoken Jessie was moving to his side. They stood for a moment gazing out the glass panes toward the town. The red spurts of muzzle-blast still broke the night's darkness, and they could hear the muffled sounds of gunfire.

"I'm not sure that the marquis will want our help, or need it," she said. "But I think we'd better volunteer to lend him a hand in case he does."

"Of course," Ki agreed.

They turned away from the door, but even when the heavy drapes fell back across it they could still hear the faint noises of the gunfire. Jessie bent over her valise and took out her Colt, holstered for traveling, its gunbelt rolled around the holster. She buckled on the gunbelt as she and Ki hurried to the door and went downstairs.

De Mores was hastening through the hallway that bordered the stairs as Jessie and Ki reached the chateau's main floor.

"Do not alarm yourselves, please," he said when he saw them. "This has occurred before, and I am prepared to deal with it. After the first attack by these villainous night-shooters I gave orders to every man who works on my estate to saddle horses and bring their weapons at once any time of the day or night when they hear gunfire."

"Ki and I aren't strangers to fighting," Jessie told him. "If we can help you—"

"My men should be here any moment," the marquis replied without breaking stride as he hurried along the wide, thickly carpeted hallway. "I am going to the gunroom now to get my own rifle. We will help the people in Medora."

"Would you object if we go with you?" Jessie asked. "I'm a reasonably good shot, and neither Ki nor I frighten easily. I don't have anything but my Colt, but—"

"I will not be ungracious and refuse your offer, Miss Starbuck," de Mores broke in as he opened the door of a room facing the corridor. "If you desire a rifle, please feel free to select one from my gunrack. And you may choose one as well, Mr. Ki, if you choose to join us."

"Thank you, Marquis, but I carry my own weapons," Ki responded. "But I'll certainly go along with you and help fight, whoever the attackers might be."

While they talked they had gone through the door de Mores opened, and he struck a lucifer to light the lamps that stood on small tables just inside the room, on each side of the entry.

Jessie gasped when she saw the array of weapons in the small chamber. Both side walls were lined with cabinets that had been fitted with special racks. Only one of the cabinets contained pistols, and these were few in number

100

compared to the sporting rifles and shotguns that rested upright on the specially fitted shelves. Jessie was not an expert on firearms, but at several times before Alex's death she had gone with him to visit the homes of some of his wealthy industrialist and banking friends who were gun collectors.

In the open-faced cabinets she recognized many of the weapons as the products of Europe's most famous arms-makers. The guns of Deleomyer of Belgium, Deaudeteau and de Gras and Martini-Henry of France, Vetterli of Italy, Westly-Richards of England, and Sharps and Winchester of the United States were represented among the rifles and shotguns.

At any other time, Jessie might have paid more than casual attention to the shotguns and pistols, for in the quick glance she'd given to the cabinets in which handguns rested in fitted compartments she'd noted several ancient single-shot dueling pistols in addition to weapons she recognized as the creation of Samuel Colt and Henry Deringer, as well as Webley, Smith & Wesson, Mauser and de Gras. Now, however, she moved swiftly along the racks of varied weaponry looking for a familiar weapon.

"You have quite a choice of weapons, Marquis," she commented as she moved in front of the gleaming long guns until she came to a trio of Winchester rifles and reached for the one which was the same model as her own.

"Weaponry is a fancy of mine," de Mores answered. He had also ignored the handguns and was holding a Martini-Henry rifle. "But I see that you have made your choice. You will find ammunition for it in the drawer below the cabinet."

On the heels of de Mores's remark, one of the men who'd been in the retinue that met her and Ki at the train came in. He clicked his heels military-style and bobbed a

101

half-bow as he said, "We are ready, Excellency, whenever you wish to start."

"Horses?" de Mores asked.

"Are at the door," the man replied. "But I did not know that your guests would be joining us."

"See to horses for them, then," the marquis snapped. "And hurry, or we will not arrive until the fighting is over."

Almost before the marquis had finished his remark, a rifle barked at close range. The bullet tore through the draperies of the window, whistled as it sped across the room, and plowed with a sullen *thunk* into the inner wall. Shots in reply came from outside, followed by a second ragged volley and the harsh grating of slugs on the stone walls of the building.

"They are attacking us!" the servant gasped.

"So it seems." de Mores nodded as he started toward the window. As he moved he was feeding shells into the magazine of the rifle he'd selected. "My men will not return until we have set the attackers to flight. I've spent many hours instructing them in the methods of combat."

Leaving Ki to make his own choice, Jessie wasted no time. She pulled open the drawer that de Mores had indicated and found shells for the rifle she'd selected, then joined her host at the window. Shouldering the Winchester, she began swinging it slowly from side to side while she scanned the darkness, waiting for a target.

Her target appeared sooner than she'd expected. In an almost direct line with the sights of her slowly-moving rifle a spurt of muzzle-blast broke the night's black gloom. Jessie reacted instantly. She corrected her aim while the point from which the spurt of red had come was still fresh in her mind and bracketed the spot with three quick, closely-spaced shots. She could not be sure, amid the general confusion of the attack, but thought that over the shooting

102

she'd heard a yell of pain from the area at which she'd aimed.

While searching the darkness with her eyes, trying to locate another of the night riders, she slipped her hand into her pocket and took out three fresh cartridges to replace the rounds she'd fired. She watched the black gloom beyond the window darkness for a moment, looking for another opportunity, but the shots now seemed to be coming from the edges of the area which a few minutes earlier had been broken almost incessantly by the muzzle-blasts.

In the earliest stages of the attack Jessie had been too busy arming herself and loading the rifle she'd chosen to count the number of attackers by watching the spurts of flame coming from their weapons, but now she began keeping a mental tally, noting the number of different points from which the bursts of red were coming. She counted seven, none of them from places that she could cover quickly enough to respond. While she was trying to locate a fresh target, other, more distant shots began sounding from the opposite side of the chateau.

Beside Jessie, de Mores was firing carefully aimed shots, shifting his rifle with calm deliberation each time a fresh spurt of muzzle-blast punctured the darkness. Jessie quickly followed his example, holding her rifle to her shoulder, gazing at the outside gloom until a flare of muzzle-blast spurted through the blackness, then loosing a quick shot at the spot where the red tongue of flame suddenly appeared.

She glanced around once in search of Ki, but he was no longer in the room. Jessie continued to let off her carefully aimed shots without worrying. She knew that Ki had small regard for firearms and did not use them unless circumstances forced him to do so. He relied on his skill at the *ninja* approach to an enemy and the silent but deadly whirling blade of a *shuriken*.

Shouts were being raised in the black night now, and Jessie took them as an indication that the marquis's man-servants had joined the fray, for she saw muzzle-blasts close to the walls of the chateau.

"My servants have joined us against the intruders," de Mores commented as casually as though he were giving Jessie the time of day. "If you prefer to stay here, by all means do so; but I must join the men outside."

Jessie nodded and said, "I'll go along, if you don't mind. If the odds are against the attackers, they may decide to give up, and I wouldn't want to lose a chance to speed them up with a few rifle bullets."

She followed de Mores down the hallway to the wide entrance door. One of the twin portals was ajar, and the marquis opened its twin to allow a broad beam of light to spill from the hall across the narrow veranda and the broad steps that led to the ground.

As he opened the door, de Mores said, "I will go to the left as we descend the steps—that is the direction from which out attackers are firing. Perhaps you might choose to go toward the opposite side, in the event that they choose to retreat in that direction."

Though Jessie recognized the suggestion as a device to keep her from being exposed to danger, and had no intention of doing as the marquis had suggested, she nodded. They went swiftly down the short flight of steps and de Mores moved to the left with long unhesitating steps.

Jessie took a few short steps to her right into the dense darkness that bordered the wide swathe of light from the open double doors. Safely shrouded from casual observation in the gloom, she stopped for a moment to get her bearings. There was no noise of shooting now from the direction which de Mores had suggested that she take, but from the side of the chateau they'd been covering from the gunroom window, the shooting had not slackened. The rifle barks were spaced farther apart now, and the voices of men calling to one another in the darkness could be heard more often.

Footsteps scraping on the gravel of the driveway that arced in front of the steps drew Jessie's attention to the shooting that was still going on around the chateau. Its volume was more intense than ever now, and she realized from the number of weapons now being discharged that the household's manservants had joined the fight.

From her new position in front of the chateau Jessie could see only two or three of the red blasts that broke the night when one of the attackers fired. She realized quite well that in the dark it would now be very difficult to distinguish between friend and foe. Listening carefully, she tried to separate the sources of the firing by the location and sound of their discharge, but the blackness of both sides of the swathe of light streaming from the mansion's open door was as deep as ever.

Though she could still see an occasional spurt of flame break the gloom, there was no way for her to tell whether it came from the rifle of one of the attackers or had been triggered by one of the marquis's men. Frustrated by the darkness that crippled her ability to act, Jessie started to turn back and go into the house.

She now realized that while it might be possible for the marquis and his men to recognize one another even in the pitch darkness, she could only shoot blindly at muzzle-blasts. The only way for her to distinguish friend from foe was to return to the gunroom. There, looking down on the grounds, she could tell by the spreading pattern of a gun's muzzle-blast whether the shooter was facing the chateau and shooting at it, or had his back to the building and was aiming at the night riders.

Turning, Jessie started back toward the open door. She'd reached the steps and was lifting her foot to start up them when a loud, high-pitched yell rang out behind her. It came from the darkness beyond the wide, spreading light spilling from the doorway. Acting in response to reflexes honed to a fine edge by the battles she and Ki had waged with the cartel before smashing it, Jessie turned. As she moved she lowered her rifle, holding it at waist level with her left hand while her right swooped down to the butt of her Colt.

Then she saw the man who'd loosed the yell as he came into the fan of light spreading from the open doors. Her hand stopped suddenly, grasping the butt of her revolver, as he looked up at her and the light from the doorway showed his face.

What Jessie saw was an apparition from the past. The man who'd appeared so unexpectedly was standing in the flood of light, looking at her. He wore a long, black frock coat that fell to his knees and a hat of the style favored by trappers and plainsmen of an earlier day. The hat had a flattened crown which fitted his head closely, and a wide, straight brim that shaded his eyes and cheekbones in spite of the wavy warps that distorted it.

All that Jessie could see of his eyes below the wide brim of his hat was the glinting they reflected from the light that spilled from the doorway. However, she could make out quite clearly the portion of his thin face that was not hidden by the shadow of his hatbrim. He had an overlong straight nose with high, flared nostrils that touched the thick straggling blond moustache which descended in a frizzy but straight sweeping spread past the corners of his lips and

106

slanted down below his jawline on both sides. She could also see that his light, wavy hair dropped to his shoulders on both sides of his head.

Though twin ivory-grip Colt revolvers were holstered at his hips on a gunbelt buckled on outside his frock coat, the new arrival made no move to draw. He stood for a moment gazing up at Jessie, then brought up his right hand very slowly and touched the brim of his hat. He held his arm raised, partly shielding his face and throwing it into shadow as he spoke.

"You ain't got a thing to worry about from me, ma'am," he said. "Wild Bill don't draw on ladies or children."

Dropping his hand as he turned, the man took off at a run. The first two steps he took carried him out of sight. He was gone in an instant, swallowed by the darkness that shrouded the front of the chateau.

Although Jessie was usually impervious to surprise, she stood for a moment in stunned amazement as she stared into the black night at the point where the apparition had disappeared. Then she exhaled the breath she'd been holding since her first glimpse of the man who'd just vanished.

"It can't be!" she said aloud. "It's impossible!"

Red muzzle-blast spurted from the darkness, and the crack of a shot broke Jessie's dazed spell as did the bullet that sang past her and thunked into the wall of the chateau above her head. Moving more by instinct than by force of will, she brought up the Winchester in a flashing move and triggered off a shot at the spot where the streak of red had flashed. There was no answering shot, and she hurried to carry out her original intention of returning to the gunroom, where she'd at least have a chance of finding a target or two.

By the time Jessie reached the gunroom, it was obvious

to her that the attackers were withdrawing. Shots from the darkness sounded less often now. The muzzle-flashes broke the gloom only infrequently, and rarely did a stray bit of lead thunk against the chateau's stone walls.

She was standing gazing into the gloom outside, still frustrated by lack of any target, when the soft whisper of silk reached her ears and she turned to face Medora de Mores.

"I was curious," the marquise said. "The shooting seems to be stopping on the side of the chateau that my suite faces."

"Yes, the men who've been attacking are apparently pulling away," Jessie replied. "But from what the marquis said, this isn't the first time your home has been attacked. Tell me, how many times have they been here before?"

"This is their third visit," her hostess answered. "The first time they took us quite by surprise. Antoine expected a second attack, and was prepared for it, just as he was for this one tonight."

By this time the sound of shots no longer reached them. Jessie listened for a moment before saying, "I'm sure he's tried to find out who they are, and what's behind their moves?"

"Of course. Glass is too hard to replace here in the Dakota Territory for us to allow them to continue their harassment. But my belief is that Antoine is right; there must be some connection between the attacks and his plant in the town."

"He told me that a large number of the men working in the plant are Indians," Jessie said, frowning. "Most of them Sioux, I believe he said. Could he have done something that they would take as being offensive to their gods?"

"Who can say?" The marquise shrugged. "I know too little about the redskins even to guess." A puzzled expression crossed her face. She paused, then went on, "The idea had not occurred to me, Miss Starbuck, and I'm not aware that Antoine has ever considered it. I must mention it to him—or perhaps you should."

"It might be better coming from you," Jessie suggested.

"Yes. Very well, I'll mention it to him later."

Voices and footsteps sounded outside the room, and in a moment de Mores came in, with Ki close behind him.

"We've driven them off again, and without any greater trouble than before," the marquis said. "But this harassment becomes tiresome. I must find out what—or who— is behind it."

"Perhaps it's just a diversion, to keep you from helping the people in the village," Ki suggested. "There must be some connection."

"Of course." De Mores nodded. "But they have done no more damage to the plant than they have here at the chateau."

"Miss Starbuck has asked me if you have done anything that might offend the redskins," the marquise said. "Or some of the gods to which the savages pray."

"A very astute suggestion, Miss Starbuck," the marquis said, turning to face Jessie. "I will ask some questions."

"And there's something else that I hadn't gotten around to mentioning while the marquise and I were talking," Jessie told him. "I had quite a surprise just before the attackers stopped shooting and withdrew. It was just after you'd left, Marquis."

"A surprise?" De Mores frowned. "Of what nature?"

"When you went to join your men, I stayed at the entrance for a few minutes, deciding which way I should move," Jessie replied. "And before I could make up my mind I saw one of the strangest sights I've ever encountered. I suddenly found myself looking at—well, I don't like to appear superstitious, but I'm prepared to swear that I saw the ghost of Wild Bill Hickok."

Chapter 10

Ki broke the silence that followed Jessie's announcement. "That's impossible!" he exclaimed. In his surprise he even abandoned his customary habit of speaking softly, and raised his voice excitedly. "You know as well as I do that Wild Bill Hickok's dead, Jessie! He was killed almost ten years ago, right here in the Dakota Territory!"

"Of course I know that, Ki!" Jessie replied. "But for the past half hour I've been trying to decide how positive I am that he really is dead. And I—"

"A moment, Mademoiselle Starbuck," de Mores broke in. "My apologies for interrupting. If you indeed saw this Wild Bill Hickok, then who is buried in the grave I have seen with his name on the tombstone?"

"I've heard about his death, of course, Marquis, and never have doubted until tonight that what I heard was true. But I've also heard of the deaths of other people, and found that what I'd believed true had been exaggerated."

111

Jessie spoke very calmly, but her brows knitted with perplexity as she tried to separate truth from speculation while she was speaking. "Tonight, I saw a man who was either Wild Bill Hickok himself, or someone who looked enough like him to be his twin."

As Ki listened to Jessie, a puzzled frown had also formed on his face. He asked her, "Do you have any doubt that you weren't just mistaking a chance resemblance, Jessie?"

"It wasn't a chance resemblance, Ki," she replied. "You remember that both of us saw Hickok several times during that year we went to New York with Alex. And Wild Bill Hickok wasn't a man—or maybe I should say *isn't*—a man you'd forget."

"That's right," Ki agreed. "I remember thinking how impressive he was while I listened to him trying to persuade Alex to invest in a Wild West show he'd started in Niagara Falls."

"During the month we were in New York, he came to the hotel at least three times to see if he could change Alex's mind," Jessie went on. "And almost a year after that, when his show at Niagara Falls had gone bankrupt, Hickok came all the way to the Circle Star, hoping Alex would finance him in a new Wild West show that he could take on a world tour."

"Yes, I'd forgotten about that." Ki nodded. "His visit was during the spring gathers, and I was staying out on the range with the hands, so I didn't see him that time."

"Even if the light I saw him in tonight wasn't very good, I recognized him at once, or was sure I did," Jessie said. "It gave me such a spooky feeling that all I could do was stand there gaping while he looked at me for a minute before he moved into the dark and I lost sight of him."

"This man you took to be Hickok, did he say anything?" de Mores asked Jessie.

"Only a few words, something to the effect that he didn't fight women," Jessie answered. "I was still staring at him, and before I could move closer to him, he walked off into the dark."

"Did this man you thought to be Hickok threaten you in any way?" de Mores asked.

Jessie shook her head. "No. Quite the opposite, Marquis. Just before he walked away he said something about Wild Bill not threatening women or children, or shooting at them."

"This is indeed something new." Medora de Mores frowned. "Antoine, you must look into it. Who can tell what our enemies may be planning?"

"Have no fear, my dear," the marquis replied. "If Miss Starbuck and Ki are not too exhausted after the disturbance we have just had, coming so soon after their arrival, I am planning to take them to the factory tomorrow. To combine two visits into one, I shall give them a chance to look at the town as well. I will certainly ask some questions while we are in both places."

Except for the occasional glint of a spent brass cartridge on the thinly-grassed ground, there were no signs of the night's raid as Jessie and Ki rode beside the marquis on the way to the slaughtering plant the following morning. For reasons he did not explain to them, the marquis had led them north from his chateau instead of taking the rutted wagon road they'd used when they'd first arrived. Jessie and Ki had exchanged puzzled frowns when de Mores had first turned his horse's head away from the wagon trace, but had asked no questions. After they'd covered perhaps half the distance to the river, de Mores pointed to what

113

they'd taken to be a smudge of low clouds still farther north.

"My sheep herd," he announced. "More than a thousand head. They will provide wool which can be sold to the spinning mills. Because the sheep is a prolific animal, as the herd grows I will also be able to pass them through my meat plant and send a goodly number to the market as mutton."

Jessie's voice was without enthusiasm as she replied, "Yes, I suppose this part of the Dakota Territory is too dry to support cattle."

"Not so, Miss Starbuck!" de Mores protested. "On my land to the south there are green valleys, and streams that flow even in the heat of summer. That is where I keep my cattle. It is a small herd now, only six hundred head, but it will grow just as the sheep herd will."

"And provide carcasses for your meat plant, too," Ki said.

"Of course!" de Mores agreed. "You see, I have thought of everything."

"You really do have a much more extensive operation here than I'd imagined," Jessie said thoughtfully. "Jason Maxwell didn't do it justice in describing it when he suggested that I stop and look at it on the way back to Texas."

"Mr. Maxwell has been very helpful," the marquis replied. "But in spite of his help I still find myself in need of more capital, Miss Starbuck. The war in Europe has reduced the income on which I have relied to sustain my enterprises here until they become self-sustaining."

Jessie said nothing. Because of the Starbuck name, she'd been offered many investments in many fields since Alex's death. She'd refused most of them, for the example set by him was very strong. Her father's foundation for the vast fortune he'd accumulated and passed on to her had not been acquired by flights of fancy into still-untested fields such as those which the Marquis de Mores was entering. Especially in his beginning days, Alex Starbuck had for the most part confined his activities to the careful purchase of businesses in the basic industries which were floundering because of mismanagement, and correcting the problems which were causing their troubles.

When Jessie did not respond to de Mores's hint, he went on, "There will be an immense return from my ventures here, I am convinced of that. Perhaps you will wish to discuss the growth I foresee for them, after you have seen for yourself how practical they will be as the country grows."

"Perhaps." Jessie nodded. "But I'll have to see first just how well your ideas are working out."

"Certainement," he agreed, looking ahead along the trail they had been following since passing the sheep herd. "We are very close to the river now; we will ride along its bank to the ford below the railroad bridge and go first to my beef plant."

"It looks a great deal bigger when you get inside than it does when you pass it on the train," Ki commented to Jessie.

They had stopped just inside the door of the marquis's beef factory. De Mores had left them there to wait, after explaining apologetically that he needed to confer briefly with his foreman, to find out if the plant had suffered any damage from the mysterious night attack.

Throughout the interior of the huge brick building, all but a few of the workers—most of them, Jessie noted, Indians—worked stripped to the waist. Some wore the fringed buckskin leggings that were the common attire of the northern tribes, but a handful were clad only in breech-clouts.

Almost everywhere that Jessie and Ki looked the scene was one of incessant activity. Men hurried here and there, some pushing large carts that carried an entire steer carcass, others busy at butchering stations which were located at intervals along the interior of the cavernous structure.

"It's on a big scale, all right," Jessie commented. "But I suppose it would have to be. And I still wonder whether all the activity we're seeing results in a profit."

"That's the key, of course," Ki agreed. "But here comes the marquis. I think our tour is about to begin."

De Mores came up to them and stopped. He indicated the far end of the building with a gesture and said, "We must start at the beginning, Miss Starbuck. Only then will you understand what I have accomplished here."

"I'm always interested in seeing something new," Jessie said. Then she asked, "But before we start, did the man you were talking to have anything to say about the attack on the town last night?"

"It seems to have been of the same nature as the one made on the chateau, something of a gesture." De Mores frowned. "I must confess that I do not understand why the night riders made such a short and meaningless visit, unless it was to alarm us."

"And I don't suppose anybody in the town saw Wild Bill Hickok—or his ghost?" Ki asked.

"No. And this is another matter I do not understand," de Mores replied, his frown deepening. "But come, let us begin." Turning back to Jessie, he went on, "If there is anything that you wish to know as we move along, I will try to explain it to you, Miss Starbuck."

"I'm very interested in looking at it," Jessie told him. "And I'm also somewhat surprised at this huge building."

They had reached the end of the cavernous structure by this time, and were gazing down its full length. The building was flooded with light, not only from its high-set windows but from wide double doors at each end. From pens just outside the door, cattle were being driven in by Sioux warriors carrying truncated lances to use as prods.

A brick paved area extended from the entrance. At its edge the steers were herded into a single line which took them to the edge of the brick, where a husky Indian swinging a heavy sledgehammer dropped them with a swinging blow between their horns. Three more of the Sioux workers were always waiting when the animal slumped in death. Together they dragged the carcass to a brick-lined gutter through which blood flowed in a steady stream.

With a single swift stroke one of the workers slashed the dead animal's throat, and as its blood gushed into the gutter one man chopped off its tail and hooves. Others were waiting with a low-slung flatbed cart to wheel the carcass along a line of waiting workers. At each step in the cleaning process the cart stopped only long enough to allow the man responsible for the next operation to do his job.

At the first station the carcass was skinned and its hide tossed into a waiting cart while still another of the Sioux workers gutted the carcass and dumped the intestines into a trough. Plunging their arms up to the elbows in offal, the men stationed at the trough removed liver, heart and tripes. Meanwhile, the cart bearing the carcass had moved on to the next work station, where in quick succession butchering details of one or two men decapitated the carcass and passed the head to still another knife wielder, who took out the tongue and brain.

At the same time the crew at the next work-station were scraping clean the cavity of the butchered steer. As each operation took place the retained organs were placed on

117

trays, which were removed at intervals and fresh trays set to replace them.

At the end of the killing and cleaning line three men took charge of the carcass. Two of them grabbed the fore-legs of the cleaned animal while a third sawed along its backbone from neck to hindquarters. The half-carcasses were then trundled to a boxcar waiting on the siding, where they were spooned together for shipment on racks from which the halves hung on huge hooks.

"Only one thing is lacking," de Mores said as they got to the end of the preparation line. He had walked beside Jessie and Ki along the line of workers, explaining each step in the process. "There is no ice to preserve the meat closer than Duluth, in Minnesota. There, when Lake Superior freezes around its shores, men saw ice into great blocks and haul it to barns. My shipments must all go there first to have ice packed around them, or the beef will spoil before it reaches Chicago or St. Louis."

"Is that as far as you ship?" Jessie asked.

"Not always. During the winter months, when the meat stays chilled in the railroad cars, I fill orders from more distant places."

"Isn't it too cold to work here in this big place in winter?" Ki frowned.

"To keep warm, my workers must stay busy," the Frenchman replied with a smile. Then he grew serious and went on, "But mine do not fear the cold. As you have seen, most of them are Sioux, though a few are Blackfoot or Ojibway. This is their native range; they are accustomed to cold weather."

"That would make a difference." Jessie agreed. "But I'm a bit curious about the size of your shipments to the East. How many sides of beef can you get into one car?"

"Seventy, at the least. Often a few more, but rarely less."

"And I can't load even half that many live steers into a cattle car when I send my Circle Star herds to market," Jessie said thoughtfully. "You should do well with your new venture, Marquis."

"I expect to," he replied, then went on, "but I can see now that it has some flaws."

"It seems to be operating very smoothly," Jessie said.

"In the plant, yes. My worries are of such matters as shipping the meat to market. If a carload of my beef is left to stand very long waiting to be attached to a train, or through some mistake made by the railway workers, the meat will spoil. In the hot weather, some will spoil if there is not enough ice placed in the car."

"How often does that happen?"

"More often than I care to contemplate."

"You're losing money, then?" she guessed.

"*C'est vrai.*" De Mores nodded. "My beef factory is not now as profitable as I had expected, but the problems which I am encountering can be cured in time."

Jessie was surprised at the marquis's frankness. Most of the men who came to her looking for loans or stock purchases to salvage an unprofitable business venture tried to gloss over their problems.

De Mores went on, "Bankers have small imaginations, Miss Starbuck. That is why Jason Maxwell suggested I talk with you."

"Yes. Jason was frank with me in suggesting that I look at your venture as a potential investment."

"And now that you've seen my beef factory, do you agree with him?"

"I'm not sure yet. I'll have to look at your account books before I can answer you."

119

"That can be easily arranged," the marquis said. "They are in my study at the chateau."

"Let's leave the matter open." Jessie went on. "We can talk about it later. Right now, I'm still very curious about the attack we fought off last night, and the one made on the town. I'd like to find out if anyone else has seen the man I took for Wild Bill Hickok last night."

"Then let me suggest that after we have talked with some of the people in Medora, we visit an Indian called Wrong Hand," the marquis said.

"Is he one of the leaders of the Sioux?" she asked.

"No. He's not a chief, but one of their medicine men. I have—shall we say, an arrangement with him."

"He's your informer?"

"I must know what the Indians who work for me in the factory can be expected to do," de Mores explained. "They do not live by the same calendar we observe. I cannot risk them failing to show up for work because of some holiday of their own, so Wrong Hand keeps me abreast of such things. If there is any talk among the Sioux of Hickok's ghost, he will surely have heard it."

Medora, the town established by the marquis and named for his wife, still bore the signs of its newness. Only a handful of its thirty or forty houses—most of them small one- and two-room shanties—had been painted. Even the store they passed on the way to visit the Sioux medicine man had walls of raw pine that still glowed with newness. The board houses were far outnumbered by the Indian tipis, which, in addition to girding the town like a loosely drawn and somewhat twisted belt, were scattered among the frame dwellings.

There were few people on Medora's crooked, narrow, dirt streets, but whenever they encountered one de Mores reined in to ask about the night attack. None of them had heard of anyone who'd been wounded, and none seemed unduly aroused or alarmed. They appeared to accept the night riders as one of the hazards of everyday living on the frontier. De Mores led Jessie and Ki on a zigzag course, winding in and out between the town's dwellings, to an isolated tipi on one of the low-rising hillocks that predominated the surrounding landscape.

A man was sitting in front of the tipi. He was wrapped in a blanket, his head bowed forward, and as they drew closer Jessie could see that his eyes were closed and he was apparently asleep. He stirred when she and her companions were within a dozen yards of the conical tent, and he looked at them for a moment, his wrinkled brown face totally expressionless. His features did not change when Jessie and Ki and de Mores reined in.

"Good morning, Wrong Hand," the marquis said. The old Sioux nodded and grunted, but did not reply. De Mores fumbled in a pocket and took out a half-dollar. He handed it to the Indian, saying, "A small gift for you."

With another nod, the Indian took the coin. Jessie understood how he'd gotten his name when she noticed he'd extended his left hand to accept the marquis's offering. He stared at de Mores for a moment, then said, "You want to know about shooting last night. The ones who attacked were the same who shot at you before. It was not my people. They have no quarrel with you, and they do not shoot before they aim."

"I know that," de Mores replied. When the old man nodded without speaking, the marquis persisted. "You're sure they're the same men?" Wrong Hand nodded, but did not speak. When the marquis saw that his question was not going to be answered, he asked, "And you still do not know where they came from?"

"I know no more than you do," the old man said.

For a moment the marquis waited. Then he went on, "All of them were the same? Was there a man called Hickok among them?"

Again Wrong Hand hesitated. At last he said, "There was one who has not shot with them before. But he is like all the others; he does not aim, either."

Jessie could not wait for the marquis to continue his questions. She broke in to ask, "Was his name Hickok?"

For a moment she thought the old Sioux was not going to answer her impulsive question, and apparently Ki did also, for after waiting for the Indian's reply Ki said, "The man we are asking about is called Bill by those he rides with."

"I heard no names called," Wrong Hand finally answered. "And here in my tipi no bullets came close."

Before Jessie could finish framing another question, de Mores broke in. "I would like to know more about these men, Wrong Hand, but I have told you this before."

"I cannot say what I do not know," the medicine man replied after a thoughtful silence. "And I do not know this thing you ask."

As soon as Wrong Hand had finished speaking, he pulled the blanket down to cover his face. De Mores turned to Jessie with a frustrated shrug.

"He will not speak with us any longer," he said. "He's treated me and others this way before. We will be wasting our time if we try to get him to say anything more. I suggest that we return to the chateau. After dinner, if you are not too exhausted, we will talk again about my factory."

★

Chapter 11

"From the way you and the marquis were talking this afternoon, I got the impression that you're thinking seriously about investing in his butchering factory," Ki said to Jessie.

They were relaxing before dinner in the sitting-room of their suite on the second floor of the chateau, resting after their long day in the saddle.

"I've been asking myself questions about it since we went through it, Ki. There's no question but that it's the logical way to get beef to market, and it has never occurred to me until now that we're shipping a tremendous lot of extra weight and bulk to market with our Circle Star herds."

"Oh, there's no question about it being a good idea. I've been thinking about it, too, asking myself what your father's reaction might've been."

"Yes, I've tried to look at it through his eyes, too. And I've also been thinking about that swindling broker in Fort

Worth who robbed the Circle Star just as effectively as though he'd put a gun to my head and demanded about sixty thousand dollars in cash."

"But you haven't yet made up your mind." Ki's words were a statement rather than a question.

Jessie shook her head. "I will soon, though. After I've seen some of his figures in black and white, I'll—" Jessie broke off as a light tapping sounded on the door.

Ki moved to answer the knock. He opened the door, Medora de Mores stood in the corridor. "I hope I'm not disturbing Miss Starbuck," she said. "But I—"

Jessie interrupted to say, "Do come in, Marquise. You're not disturbing us in the least. We were just chatting while we waited for the dinner chime."

"We'll be dining a bit later than usual this evening," the marquise said as she came into the room. "Some problem has come up in the kitchen. The cook's just sent word about putting our dinner back a half-hour or so, and I thought that would give us time for a little chat, to get better acquainted."

"I'd enjoy talking with you," Jessie replied. "I'd like to hear more about how you and the marquis decided to come here to the prairie instead of living in some large city like New York or Chicago. Do sit down."

Ki said, "If you ladies are going to talk about social life, I'll excuse myself." He went out, closing the door.

"Large cities lost their attraction for me long ago," the marquise told Jessie as she settled beside her on the divan. The lamplight was reflected now in her brilliant red hair, which was puffed out in the new pompadour fashion. She went on, "I was born and brought up in New York. From what Antoine has told me about your father, he might have been acquainted with my own father. Did you ever hear him mention the name Von Hoffman?"

"Are you speaking of the banker?" Jessie asked. When Medora nodded, Jessie went on, "Of course Alex knew him, and mentioned him often. Mr. Von Hoffman was one of the first New York bankers to underwrite his brokerage house when Alex began expanding his interests on the East Coast."

"It's too bad Father isn't alive today," the marquise said with a gusty sigh. "You see, Antoine counted on him to help in the financing of his cattle-slaughtering plan."

"Your family doesn't have an interest in the bank now?"

Medora shook her head. "I tried to persuade my family to hold on to our interest in the bank, but they preferred not to."

"And your husband is feeling a pinch, now that he doesn't have the bank behind him?"

"You're very astute, Miss Starbuck. Our situation would be different if there wasn't this threat of another war between France and England. So much of Antoine's capital funds are tied up in Europe. . . ."

"I think I understand," Jessie said as her companion's voice trailed off. "But I haven't made up my mind whether I want to invest in it, in spite of my interest in cattle ranching."

"Then do keep your mind open until Antoine can discuss the idea with you again," Medora said.

"I intend to," Jessie promised. "Now, let me ask you a question."

"Of course."

"Do you remember any occasion since you have been in the West when your husband encountered the man they called Wild Bill Hickok?"

"You're referring to the man who spoke to you during the raid on the chateau last night?"

125

"Yes. I was too surprised to do anything but stare, and I assure you that I don't often get surprised."

"Certainly Mr. Hickok's name is well-known everywhere we've been in America," Medora replied. "But when you told Antoine of your encounter last night I was quite surprised myself. I've always understood that Mr. Hickok was killed several years before we built the chateau here."

"Then someone must be using his name, perhaps to frighten you," Jessie said.

"I have no idea who it could be." The marquise frowned. "I don't even have any idea how to begin finding out."

"Neither do I, at the moment," Jessie told her. "But now my curiosity's aroused, and if you don't object to having Ki and me extend our visit a few days longer, I intend to try and find out who it is, and who's behind him."

"My dear Miss Starbuck, you're welcome to stay as long as you wish," Medora replied. "And I hope that you won't give up in your determination. *Le bon Dieu* knows that Antoine has enough problems. He should not be compelled to deal with another, whether it is a real killer or a ghost!"

Feeling at loose ends after leaving Jessie and Medora de Mores, Ki went down the stairs to the main floor of the chateau. For a moment he stood idly at the foot of the steps, trying to decide whether to go outdoors for a stroll or to return to the gunroom and take a closer look at the marquis's array of weapons than time had allowed him the previous evening. He decided on the gunroom, and was turning to go down the corridor when a woman's voice from the staircase stopped him.

"Are you looking for something or someone, Mr. Ki? If you are, maybe I can help you."

Turning, Ki glanced up the steps. The tall young woman who'd shown him and Jessie to their suite the previous evening was standing halfway down the staircase. He'd seen only her back while she was leading them down the hall, and had gotten no more than a glimpse of her face when he passed her while going through the door, which she'd closed as soon as he and Jessie were inside.

"I'm not sure you remember me," she went on. "You and your mistress must've been right tired when I showed you to your rooms last evening."

"We were a bit tired from the long train ride," Ki said. "But that's never affected my memory. I didn't learn your name, though I remember you're the marquise's personal maid."

"It's Bliss Blossom, Mr. Ki."

"Just plain 'Ki,' please," he told her. "I work for Miss Starbuck, just the way you work for the marquis and his wife. And I don't really need any help at the moment. I'm just trying to decide whether to go to the gunroom and have another look at the marquis's weapons or go outside and stroll around in the fresh air."

"It's nice outside at this time of day," she suggested. "And I've nothing to do now, what with my mistress visiting yours. If you go out for a stroll around the grounds, I could go along with you. There's not much to show you or much else to do, here in this lonesome place."

Ki took a closer look at Bliss now, attracted by the cheerful tone of her voice as well as by the statuesque figure she made. The plain one-piece serge dress she wore had a very low-cut neckline, and her full breasts bulged on either side of its deep vee. The dress had a high white collar that set off her rosy cheeks and pouting lips, and her face was framed by very light blond hair, which she wore pulled down over her ears and gathered into a roll at the back of her neck.

"Suppose we stroll outside, then," he agreed. "I haven't really seen the chateau grounds, or looked around at any of the countryside except what's between here and town."

"After you've seen the servants' quarters and stables and the granary, there's naught but little bare-top hillocks to look at," Bliss said as she started down the stairs to join Ki.

They went out into the cooling air of early evening and walked down the wide steps to the ground. The sun had not yet set, though it was very close to the horizon. The bulky chateau was casting a long dark shadow across the carefully leveled prairie that surrounded the huge building. When they'd reached the end of its facade, Bliss pointed out the buildings she'd just mentioned.

"I'm not especially interested in looking at them any closer," Ki told her. "We have about the same thing on Jessie's ranch, and I don't think I'd see anything new."

"We'll just stroll, then," she agreed. "I don't get too many chances to step out of the door even to catch a breath of fresh air, for fear the mistress will want me. I'm only going outside now because I'm sure she'll be talking with your lady for a half-hour or more and won't be needing me."

"That solves the problem for both of us, doesn't it?"

"It does that," she agreed. Then she went on, "Most of the time I stay inside. There's always something for me to do." She shot a questioning glance at Ki and asked, "What about you, though? I'd think a proper lady like Miss Starbuck would want a maid to look after her, instead of a man."

"I certainly don't do any of the things for Jessie that a

maid would," Ki replied. "She doesn't want or need anybody to look after her. I was her father's assistant before he was killed, and I do the same work for Jessie."

"So that's the way of it." Bliss nodded. "Ever since you and her got here, I've been wondering how much there was between the two of you."

"Nothing at all in the sense you're thinking of," Ki told her. "I try to be as helpful as I can without getting in her way, and she discusses her business problems with me, because I was with her father for many years and know how he'd handle matters. She doesn't always do things the way he would, but that's her affair."

"And is it true what I've heard the mistress talking with the marquis about, that your Miss Starbuck might come into his cattle-killing factory as a partner?"

"I don't know, Bliss. Jessie hasn't made up her mind what she'll do about joining with the marquis in his business."

"It's none of my affair, of course." She shrugged. "It's only talk that I've heard, and it might be better if you didn't say anything about what I've asked."

"Since it's not my affair either, I haven't any reason to mention it," Ki assured her.

While talking they'd gone along the rear of the chateau and had reached its corner. A long stretch of leveled ground lay between the building and the rough, broken terrain that stretched to the horizon. Ki could see that grass-seed had once been sown in the leveled area, but the arid air and thin soil had not been kind to the alien sprouts. Here and there a wisp of green clung precariously to life, but over most of the seeded area there were only stringy shoots, as withered and yellow as the thin arid soil.

"That was her ladyship's idea, Ki," Bliss said, indicating the aborted lawn with a sweep of her hand. "She said her family had grass all around the place where she grew up, and she wanted to see something green here."

"The Dakota Territory isn't a place to try to grow a lawn," Ki observed.

"Or much of anything else except cattle and sheep," she said, nodding. "And wild Indians."

"Do the Indians bother you?" Ki asked.

"Not a tuppence worth."

"And if I'm right, there haven't been any outlaws close by to give you any trouble," Ki went on.

"Not unless it was them that did the shooting last night and a little time ago. But up until now, it's all been quiet, too quiet for me; I like a bit of city life now and again."

Ki was reluctant to abandon the topic of the attack on the chateau. He asked, "I don't suppose the marquis has any enemies in town or on any of the ranches close by? It doesn't seem likely, since he's giving a lot of people jobs at his plant."

"If he's made enemies, last night was the first time they've showed up and shot at us. And I've never seen ghosties here."

"You have heard of Wild Bill Hickok, though?"

"A time or two. But he's a dead man, Ki! The dead don't rise from the grave and walk, or we'd be seeing them all over!"

"I'm sure you're right, Bliss. I don't believe in them myself."

They'd walked around to the front of the chateau while they were talking, and Bliss started up the steps. "I'd better get back to my own room, Ki. Her ladyship'll be needing me to help her get ready for dinner, and I'd best be there when she calls."

"We'll talk again," Ki said. "Though I don't think Jessie and I will be staying very long."

Jessie used almost the same phrase later in the evening, as she and Ki went into their suite following dinner.

"We'll only stay here one more day, Ki," she said as he closed the door of their sitting room. "I've had time to do some thinking about the marquis's plan, and I think I'll let him solve his financial problems by himself."

"What about Wild Bill Hickok, or his ghost?"

"It must be someone just using his name, trying to frighten the marquis. And there's no reason for us to go chasing after ghosts—or a man pretending to be a ghost—when there's plenty of work waiting for us at the Circle Star. I'll tell the marquis tomorrow that we're going home."

"Running a slaughterhouse is a bit out of our line." Ki nodded. "But from what I've seen, the marquis has done a very good job of planning."

"Oh, I agree with you. But I just don't think it's what I'd care to do. Now, I'm ready for a bath and bed after our day in the saddle. We'll talk about our traveling plans tomorrow."

In his bedroom, Ki made short work of undressing and slipping into bed. As always when he and Jessie were in surroundings where they had no reason to expect trouble, he went to sleep at once. He had no way of knowing how long he'd been sleeping when the click of metal roused him.

Instantly awake, Ki realized at once that what he'd heard was the faint rattle of the latch made by the door of his room as it closed. He threw back the sheet that he'd pulled up when he laid down, and reached to his bedside table, groping for the leather forearm case containing his *shuriken*. He found it at once and, moving with the efficiency of long experience, needed only seconds to slip one of the throwing blades into his hand. He was searching the gloom trying to locate the intruder when a soft whisper came from the darkness.

"Ki?" a woman's voice breathed. "It's only me."

"Bliss?" he asked, his voice also a whisper.

"Yes. Do you mind?"

Ki could see her outlined now, a vague white column in the pitch-black room. He said, "Not a bit, but I'm surprised."

"I like surprises. Don't you?"

"If they're like this one, yes."

Bliss had moved up to the bed while they were talking, and Ki could see her now. There was a momentary shimmer of light against the blackness and the whisper of cloth as she pulled her long white nightgown over her head. Then she bent over him, and for a moment her hands rustled the bed clothes as she moved them to reach his body. Then Ki felt their warmth on his chest.

"You're not all fuzzy, like some men," she whispered. "I like smooth skin better."

Bliss's hands were busy on Ki's body now, stroking down his chest to his groin. He had not yet begun an erection. Bliss fingered his limpness for a moment, her busy fingers running through his scanty pubic brush, cradling him in her palms and then squeezing him softly while her moist lips slipped over his cheeks and chin until she found his mouth.

Ki responded with his tongue when she thrust out hers, but did not allow himself to become erect. He slipped his hands down her shoulders and cupped her soft, firm breasts in his palms while he caressed their pebbled rosettes with the iron-hard tips of his fingers.

Bliss's questing hands stayed busy for several moments.

Then she broke their kiss and said huskily, "It's taking you a long time to come up."

"We're not in any hurry, are we?"

"No. But what's the matter, Ki? Don't you like me?"

"Of course I do. And I'm enjoying having you with me."

"I know something you'll enjoy more."

Bliss broke their kiss and slid her moist lips and tongue down Ki's chest, across the corded muscles of his flat abdomen. Then he felt their moist warmth as she engulfed him and began to pulse both lips and tongue in a caress that speeded his swelling. Ki enjoyed the sensation for a few minutes, continuing to brush his fingertips over her pebbled breasts while her attention brought him to fullness. Then he slipped his hands down to her waist and lifted her above him, held her suspended for a moment while he twisted them around on the yielding bed.

Bliss understood instantly what his intention was. She let herself relax while Ki lowered her to the bed, and by the time he was kneeling above her, she'd spread her thighs and was ready to accept him when Ki's rigid shaft entered her and drove deep in a smooth, full penetration.

"Ah, now, that's lovely!" Bliss gasped as he began driving in long deliberate strokes. "We've no call to hurry, Ki, and it's been a while since I've had a man like you in me! Just keep going deep and smooth, and I'll not tell you to stop!"

She sighed now and then as she brought her hips up to meet Ki's leisured rhythm, twisting her hips as he thrust, and loosing small keening cries of pleasure. Ki gauged his plunges carefully, speeding his thrusts when Bliss's soft moans of joy grew louder in her climactic moments, then slowing to a more leisured pace as she lay supine for a

133

short space, and speeding up again at the onset of her next climax.

"I've got to make a liar of myself," Bliss sighed as she shuddered out of the final throes of an especially prolonged spasm. "But you've outlasted me, Ki, and daylight must be close at hand. Just one more, now, and then we'll start afresh on a new night after I've had the day to rest."

"As you say," Ki replied without breaking his rhythmic stroking. He continued until Bliss cried out in climax, then reached his own fulfullment and lay still.

"I'll not forget tonight," Bliss breathed between her sighing gasps. "And I'll be waiting for—"

She broke off as a ragged volley of shots shattered the stillness, and Ki rose catlike to hurry to the window. He was peering outside, trying to see through the darkness when Bliss joined him.

"It's the night-riding devils again!" she said. "And I've no time to say goodbye; the marquise will be needing me!"

Ki did not turn away from the window when Bliss left, but the clicking of the door-latch told him she'd gone. He stared through the window, trying to locate the attackers and count them by the muzzle-blasts from their rifles. When he was satisfied that he'd located the four men firing at the chateau he turned away from the window and pulled on his trousers and jacket. He was groping for the leather case containing his *shuriken* when the door-latch clicked and light slivered into the room as Jessie came in. She was buckling on her gunbelt.

"They're back!" she said. "Those night-riders! Let's see if we can get close enough to them to see them in spite of the darkness, Ki. I want to find out if Wild Bill Hickok or his ghost is with them again!"

Chapter 12

"I'm ready whenever you are," Ki told Jessie. He'd slipped on his loose blouse and was slipping the *shuriken* into his vest pocket. He went on, "They're not shooting so fast this time, and I haven't heard firing from the direction of town or the slaughterhouse."

"There aren't as many attacking the chateau as there were before, either," Jessie said.

"Yes, I can tell that. I could only count four of them this time. I'm ready whenever you are."

Jessie had gone to the window and was peering into the darkness. Against the night-black sky she could see widely separated muzzle-flashes stabbing the darkness at three spots. The gunfire did not come in volleys, but as single shots fired between long intervals of inactivity.

"You're right," she agreed. "There are only four of them."

"Three on the ridge and one close to the chateau," Ki added.

Jessie went on, "And if this is the same kind of nuisance attack they made last night, it won't go on very long. But—" She paused. Then she said, "Ki, instead of joining the marquis and his men, let's saddle up and try to trail those outlaws to their hideout."

"That's a better idea than fighting them from here," Ki replied. "We can be pretty sure they won't think about us following them, and if we learn where they're holed up we'll be able to tell the marquis how he and his men can attack them."

"Or attack them ourselves." Jessie nodded. "I'm sure he'd rather stay and take charge of defending the chateau if this turns into a real attack and not just another feint."

"If they'd intended to make a real push, they'd've brought more men; but perhaps they didn't have more to bring. Last night's raid may have left them pretty badly crippled."

"I think you're right," Jessie said as they hurried down the stairway. "But even if the night-riders mean business this time, the marquis has enough men to handle them."

Even before they reached the foot of the stairs they heard shots echoing down the corridor, and instead of going outside they turned and headed for the gunroom. De Mores was at the window, a rifle in his hands, peering into the night looking for a target.

"I've been hoping you would join me," he said. "Perhaps you will keep firing from the house here. I must go to the stables and take charge of my men."

"Ki and I were talking as we came downstairs," Jessie replied. "We have an idea that—"

She was interrupted by another small, ragged hail of shots from the blackness. De Mores turned and triggered off a replying shot despite his lack of a target. When no replying volley came from the raiders he turned back to Jessie.

"What is your idea, Miss Starbuck?"

"When these night riders attacked before, they kept up their attack for a very short time," she reminded him. "Suppose Ki and I saddle up and follow them when they leave. When we've located the place where they're hiding out, you can lead your men against it. You might capture them if you did that."

"A stratagem worthy of Napoleon, Miss Starbuck!" de Mores said enthusiastically. "I'm not a military man; perhaps that's why it hasn't occurred to me! By all means, go and follow them! Take horses from my stable. I'm sure my men are gathering there; they have orders to do so."

"We don't know where these men are camped, but it can't be very far away," Jessie said. "Just hold your men here until Ki and I get back, and we'll lead you to them."

"And we will deal with them properly!" de Mores promised.

Jessie nodded. She and Ki hurried down the hall to the massive carved front door and cracked it open enough to slide outside. Darkness still held, but a dark gray strip on the eastern horizon indicated the approach of the false dawn. They hurried around the corner of the chateau, keeping the building's bulk between them and the night-riders, and ran to the stables. The men employed by the marquis were already there, sheltering from the gunfire.

"Two of you get busy at once and saddle horses for us," Jessie ordered. "The rest of you take your guns and go to the chateau. The marquis needs your help."

Recognizing the voice of authority, the handful of men scurried into action. All but the two already busy dragging saddles off the rack straggled out and started for the cha-

137

teau. The men charged with getting horses ready made quick work of their job. Widely spaced shots were still being exchanged between the marquis and the chateau's attackers when Jessie and Ki swung into their saddles and started toward the ridge where the night riders were still sending their bullets toward the big stone mansion.

By now the eastern sky was glowing with a thin rim of light, showing them that the true dawn was only a short time away. As Jessie and Ki reined their mounts toward the ridge, they were surprised to see a rider dash from its sheltering concealment and spur toward the chateau.

Had the rider and his horse been approaching from the west, he and his mount would have been invisible; for behind Jessie and Ki the darkness was still full, and when they looked back at the chateau they could make it out only as an amorphous black cube that loomed between them and the stars. The rider kept his mount at a gallop, the thunk of the horse's hoofbeats drumming faintly, drowned out now and then by the report of a shot from the attackers or the mansion, just as the muzzle-blast when a shot was fired brought a few instants of blindness to all those involved in the fracas.

"Rein in!" Jessie said quickly as the drumming hoofbeats of the approaching man grew louder. "We don't have that skyline behind us to give away our moves, and it's obvious that he hasn't seen us yet."

"I think you're right," Ki agreed. He pulled his mount up beside Jessie's and slid a *shuriken* from his pocket. "If he had, he'd either be veering away or shooting by now."

They sat in their saddles and waited. The oncoming rider did not see Jessie and Ki until a mere thirty or forty yards separated them. Then the rhythm of his horse's hoofbeats broke as he reined in, and starlight gleamed on polished steel as he dropped the reins and whipped his revolvers from their holsters.

He fired without seeming to aim, the two shots barking almost as one. Both slugs missed, cutting the air beside Jessie and Ki. For a fraction of a second the night rider was visible in the spurting red muzzle-blast, and Ki raised his arm to send his wicked blade slicing through the air toward the gunman.

"No, Ki!" Jessie snapped. "That's the man I've told you about! Whoever's posing as Wild Bill is on that horse, and I want to capture him, not kill him!"

Though only a few seconds had elapsed, the oncoming outlaw had jerked at the reins to turn his horse. Now he was galloping back toward the ridge where he'd appeared.

"How can you be sure?" Ki protested. "You couldn't have gotten a good look at him in the dark."

"I saw enough by the muzzle-blast of those two pistols he fired—not that I needed to see him at all. Letting off two shots at once that way was always Wild Bill Hickok's trademark. Whoever's on that horse is the man we're after!"

Ahead of them the hoofbeats of the fleeing gunman's horse on the rocky, hard-baked prairie soil were fading away. Ki said quickly, "We'd better move, then, or he and the others will get away from us. Until the sky's light, we've got to keep within earshot of their hoofbeats."

Straining their ears and exchanging only an occasional whispered word now and then, they kept their mounts going ahead at a slow careful pace that allowed them to move in virtual silence. In the days before the cartel had been smashed, when Jessie and Ki were so often engaged in gun battles in the darkness, their skill in the art of interpreting night sounds had been honed to a fine edge. They put this skill to good use now as they followed the horse-men moving in front of them.

At times, when the sound of hoofbeats did not reach them regularly, Jessie and Ki reined in and sat quietly listening until the mount of one of the men ahead crunched over a patch of loose rock, or grated on an outcrop of the thick stratum of solid stone that formed a solid layer beneath the thin prairie soil.

In spite of their skill, though, Jessie and Ki lost their quarry even before sunup had brightened the raw, rough badlands. The riders ahead had simply disappeared somewhere north of the town the marquis had named Medora, in the wide deep gash of a canyon that yawned in front of them, suddenly and without any warning signs that it existed. The sun had not gotten high enough yet to brighten the depths of the yawning split in the barren soil, and even though they strained their eyes they could see nothing moving in the canyon's shadowed depths.

"We've lost them," Jessie said as she and Ki reined in and looked down into the huge crevasse that split the barren soil.

"I'm afraid so," Ki agreed. "They must be down there in this canyon, though."

"Of course; it's the only place they could've gone. And all we have to do is find the trail they used."

"But we haven't heard any hoofbeats in front of us for the last twenty or thirty minutes."

"We took the only chance we had, Ki," Jessie reminded him. "And I'm sure that if we follow the canyon rim and look carefully, we'll cross their tracks somewhere close by."

"It's likely," Ki agreed. "But . . ." He paused for a long moment. Then, as Jessie kept silent, he went on, "We've done what we set out to do, Jessie. We've driven the night riders away from the chateau. Do we really need to chase them any longer?"

Now it was Jessie who hesitated and sat silently thoughtful for a few moments before replying. At last she said, "What you're really suggesting is that we don't have any personal stake in the marquis's problems, now that I've decided not to invest in his cattle marketing venture. Isn't that right?"

"It's not that I'm questioning your decision, Jessie," Ki replied. "But after we broke the cartel's back, you seemed very happy just to look after Starbuck Enterprises."

"I was. And I am," Jessie agreed. "But I suppose I do have a lot of sympathy with someone who's in the situation that we were for such a long time. It's true that we don't owe the Marquis de Mores anything, except that we were his guests when his chateau was attacked."

When Jessie paused, Ki said, "Yes, we do owe him a bit of help because of that."

"But it's not just what we'd do for a host, Ki," Jessie went on. "This business about somebody posing as Wild Bill Hickok's ghost intrigues me. It's—well, a mystery that I'd like to solve for my own personal satisfaction, even if it does involve some trouble and danger."

"I suppose that's all the answer I needed." Ki smiled. "So let's get on with tracking him. Shall we split up here and try to pick up his trail down into the canyon?"

Jessie nodded. "Yes. We both know what to do; we've been in this same situation before. I'd say an hour by the sun is a reasonable time to look."

Each of them knew without further explanation what lay ahead in rough canyon-cut country such as they'd now encountered. They'd use the methods they'd learned long ago to employ. If neither Jessie nor Ki found a trail after riding for an hour, both would turn back and they'd meet at their starting point. If one of them found a trail, whoever found it would simply stop and wait for the other to join him.

In such raw and rugged and unsettled terrain, there was little chance that there'd be two trails into the canyon with less than a half day's ride between them. The searcher who'd been unsuccessful would turn back after an hour's ride, and if the other was not waiting at the point where they separated he would ride on until encountering the one who'd stopped at the trail to the canyon floor.

"The longer we wait to start looking, the bigger lead those outlaws will have on us, so let's move right now," Ki said.

Though both Jessie and Ki were hungry, neither mentioned food. They turned in opposite directions and started riding along the canyon rim.

Jessie was riding east when she left Ki, and though the country through which she traveled was strange to her, the rugged terrain had many similarities to other parts of the unsettled West with which she was familiar.

In this part of the Dakota Territory, the land was arid, cut by gullies and dry washes. Its low-growing, thirsty vegetation was sparse and straggling. Here thick forests found no rich, well-watered soil which welcomed tree roots, and the green growth was confined to a few tough juniper bushes and scrub pines which struggled to survive along the canyon's rim. Only in the bottom where the small stream flowed, gushing briefly at snowmelt and trickling to a thread in the summer, did any real growth prosper.

Jessie flicked her eyes across the land as she rode along the canyon's brink. Most of her attention went to the canyon itself, for now and then she caught a glimpse of the stream that trickled in a narrow bed along its floor. She saw no signs to indicate that a rider had passed this way lately, and was about to turn back when a wisp of smoke rising beyond a crag which jutted above the rim caught her eye. She touched the flank of her mount with the toe of her boot, and the horse picked up its gait a bit as she started for the crag.

Ki, riding with the sun at his back and the dark, elongated shadow of his shoulders blending with the wider shadow of his horse on the dry, hard earth in front of him, moved through a landscape which differed very little from the one Jessie was encountering.

There were the same small clusters of green, an occasional scrub cedar that was little more than a twisted clump of thin green branches above a small gnarled trunk, and here and there a straggling patch of thin-stemmed grass, its seeds blown from some more fertile soil, struggling to root in the coarse, parched soil of the canyon's rim.

Once he came to an area pocked with dark dots, all that remained of ancient Indian campfires, with a few bleached shards of bone scattered on the ground around them. He turned aside from the rim long enough to ride through the old campsite, trying to determine whether any of the scattered embers were fresh. He found no signs of recent use, and no areas where the soil had been disturbed, so he resumed his slow progress along the canyon rim.

Although he watched carefully, looking for the line of pocked and broken soil which would indicate a trail, he saw nothing. From time to time he took note of the change in the shadow which moved in front of him, growing steadily shorter and more clearly defined. When the front edge of the black blob drew close to the nose of his horse, he rose in his stirrups to take a final look at the terrain ahead, and with a shrug of disappointment turned back to rejoin Jessie.

Jessie resettled her Colt in its holster as she drew closer to the crag that jutted like a tiered tower above the rim of the canyon. It was a monument to the wind, a vertical spur of nearly white rock that had been stripped of any loose particles of sand, and rose like a sculptured column at the very edge of the canyon.

Jessie was within a dozen yards of the crag before she could see the faint traces of disturbed earth that stretched away from it. The sun was high by now, and the faint, rounded pocks of hoofprints on the soil beyond the jutting monolith cast only the smallest line of shadow. The prints began beyond the crag and followed the rim of the canyon to its base, where they vanished behind it.

Reining in, Jessie studied the telltale marks. As her eyes followed them away from the crag she saw something that had been hidden before, a dark blob of horse-droppings. The small mound was still moist and glistening in the bright sunlight, and this was all the evidence she needed that a horse and its rider had passed only a short time earlier.

Almost by instinct, Jessie's hand moved to the butt of her Colt, holstered at her hip. She sat motionless for a moment, listening, but no sound broke the light, dry breeze. Her eyes on the trail, looking for fresh signs of its recent use, she nudged her horse with the toe of her boot. The animal moved ahead.

With its first steps, Jessie could see the point just beyond the towering monolith where the trail slanted down into the canyon. The soil at the edge was loose and to the eyes of an expert rider such as Jessie, very treacherous.

Looking closely, she let her reins stay slack, allowing the horse to find its own footing as it advanced.

Bootsoles grating on gravel drew Jessie's eyes from the hoofprints in the trail at the canyon's rim. Belatedly, Jessie realized that she'd made a mistake when she did not dismount and check the area on foot. A hard-faced man in dusty clothing stepped from behind the monolith. The rifle he held was aimed directly at Jessie and only a few feet away.

"Well, now," he said, a twisted but satisfied grin on his beard-bristling face. "When I seen you heading thisaway, I sorta figured you might come along this far. You just set right still, lady. If you even look like you're going to reach for that sixgun on your hip, I'll blow you outta that saddle, and it won't hurt my feelings a bit to do it."

★

Chapter 13

"Don't worry," Jessie said. "I'm not foolish enough to give you an excuse for pulling the trigger."

Her voice was calmly level as she looked at the man holding the rifle. The casual way in which he gripped its stock told her that he was a veteran at handling the weapon. Its barrel was rock-steady, and the menacing orifice of its muzzle was less than ten feet away from her. Jessie had seen at once that the distance of the muzzle was carefully calculated. The rifle was too far to enable her to strike or kick its muzzle and spoil her captor's aim, but close enough to ensure deadly aim if she tried to draw her revolver.

"I'm real glad you feel that way," he replied. His head moved only a fraction of an inch as he flicked his cold eyes over Jessie. He went on, "Just don't make no fool moves, and me and you'll get along right good. Now, the first thing you're gonna do is take that Colt outta your holster.

Lift it up with two fingers and toss it right down by my feet where I can get to it easy."

Little as she relished the command, Jessie had been sure it was coming. She had no choice but to obey. Grasping the butt of her revolver between her thumb and forefinger she swung it slowly, then let it fall in an arc that dropped the weapon only inches from her captor's boot-toe. Without taking his eyes off her, the man hunkered down and picked up the Colt. He shoved it into his belt.

"All right," he continued. "You can git off of your nag now. I don't aim for you to try no tricks while we're going down into the canyon."

"I hope you don't mind telling me why you're taking me down there," Jessie said coolly. She was half-convinced that she already knew the answer, but she wanted to be sure. "If it's my money you're after, I'll hand over the little bit I'm carrying and won't argue about it. Then I can go on my way and you can go yours."

"I'll have your money anyways," he replied, an ugly smile forming on his unshaven face. "But I ain't in that much of a hurry to git it. Anyways, I got other business with you."

"What kind of business?"

"Oh, you'll find out soon enough. Now start on down that trail. I'm gonna be right in behind you, and if you're smart as I figure you to be, you won't try to pull no funny tricks like falling down and making out like you're hurt."

Jessie turned and started down the narrow trail, her captor behind her leading her horse. Her mind was racing as she picked her way down the steep canyon wall. It was obvious that the man who'd captured her knew who she was; his words had hinted at a familiarity with her which left no doubt in her mind about that. But as far as she knew

148

all her bitter enemies within the cartel had either died or retreated to their native lands.

While she was trying to resolve the puzzle, paying too little attention to her surroundings, Jessie's foot slipped in the loose earth of the narrow trail that zigzagged down the canyon's steep wall. Looking at the almost vertical sides of the narrow gash in the desolate terrain she realized that she needed to give her full attention to the job of getting to the floor of the canyon instead of trying to solve the riddle of her capture.

She remained silent, picking her way carefully as she went down the slope until she reached a narrow strip of solid earth bordering the tiny stream she'd seen from above. Stopping at the water's edge she started to turn and face the man again, but before she'd shifted more than a few inches she stopped and stepped back with a start as he jabbed the muzzle of his rifle into her ribs.

"Turn downstream and keep moving," he commanded. "It ain't a wide trail, but you can manage it. There'll be more room a little ways up ahead. You can stop and catch your breath when we get there."

Without replying, Jessie turned and resumed her slow walk. In a few minutes the wall of the canyon curved away from the bank of the rivulet—the stream was too small and shallow to be called a river—and the path widened as they entered a small vale where the steep rise of the canyon wall began a hundred yards or more from the stream.

As small as the level spot was, it held the piled remains of what had probably been a goldseeker's cabin or shanty. About half the weathered shingles of its roof were missing, some of the wide boards forming its walls had fallen, and the entire structure had a pronounced lean that forewarned of its imminent collapse. It stood away from the riverbank, close to the steep wall. A scattering of bushes, some of them as high as Jessie's waist, dotted the raw earth between the rise of the canyon and the rivulet. A saddled horse was tethered to one of them.

"We'll stop here a minute before we mount up," Jessie's captor said. "But don't get no idea about making a run. I'd as lief shoot you as look at you."

"I'd like to know where you're taking me," she told him.

"You wouldn't know any more'n you do now," he replied. "And you'll find out soon enough anyways."

"At least tell me your name," she suggested. "If I want to tell you something or ask you something, all I can do now is call 'Hey, you.'"

For a moment he looked at her as though the suggestion surprised him. Then he said, "I don't imagine you've ever heard it before, and it don't make much never-mind, but the name's Ramley. Now, get up on that nag of yours and let's be moving along."

Jessie was wise enough not to argue. She levered herself into the saddle of her borrowed horse, wishing that the animal was Sun. On the back of the magnificent palomino stallion, her favorite mount, she might have been able to make a run for freedom. But Sun was many miles away, on the Circle Star.

In the saddle, she made no objection when Ramley lashed her wrists to the saddlehorn with a stout leather thong. She sat watching him silently while he formed the knots and tested them before going to his own horse and mounting. He freed his lasso from its saddle strap and tied it to the bridle of Jessie's mount, then levered himself into the saddle of his own horse and led the way back to the trail beside the river.

After leaving the vale where they'd stopped, the trail soon narrowed again. Though the bends in the river were a bit gentler than they'd been before, and the stream-bed broadened, the flow of water did not increase, and Jessie could see that it was now only inches deep. Every grain of sand and each rock on its bottom seemed to be visible in the light of the sun as that glowing orb now began dropping in the cloudless sky.

On both banks of the river the sides of the canyon through which it flowed rose as high and as steeply as before. Jessie scanned the canyon and stream closely as they rode, trying to remember the terrain. She was already thinking of the night ahead. Though she was positive that when she did not show up to meet Ki he would start tracking her at once, in the event that he had trouble finding her or following in the darkness the tracks she and Ramley were leaving she wanted to be prepared to help as much as she could.

She shelved her speculations and the fragments of her unformed plans when, after rounding a much longer curve than they'd yet passed in the river's course, the cliffs that rose beside them suddenly stretched back from the stream in a shoulder that created an area of flatland that she judged to be at least a half-mile wide. Scattered over the expanse of level ground that now stretched between the river and the cliffs there were a dozen or more buildings.

Only a moment of close inspection was needed for Jessie to realize that this was all that remained of a long-abandoned mining camp. None of the buildings looked imposing, in spite of the fact that two or three were bigger than the barns on most of the ranches that Jessie had seen in the territory. The others in the tumbledown array were small cabins, only large enough to accommodate a bedstead and stove.

Several of the cabins leaned at odd angles, as though they were ready to collapse completely if struck by a gust of wind. Some were so close to total deterioration that they looked ready to tumble down if a person sneezed anywhere near them. None of them had been painted, and dark streaks of rust from weathered nail-heads marked the sides of most. Two or three horses were visible between the shacks, browsing on the grassy weeds that sprouted willy-nilly between the decaying structures. A thread of smoke came from the ragged-edged chimney of one of the pair of large buildings. It was the only sign that the ghost town was still being used.

"Where are we?" Jessie asked.

"Seems to me you'd be smart enough to tell that," Ramley answered. "We've got to the place we been heading for."

"I don't have to be very smart to figure that out," Jessie retorted. "I'm sure the river over there is the Little Missouri, but doesn't this place have a name?"

"If it did, it was so long ago that everybody's forgot it." Ramley grinned. "Besides, you don't need to know anything but that it's where we are."

A shout sounded from somewhere among the scattering of cabins. "Hey, Ramley! Looks like you was right! Who you got there with you?"

"It's the Starbuck woman, Sparrow," Ramley replied.

Jessie looked around, trying to locate the man who'd started the exchange of shouts. But before she could locate him another man came out of the nearest of the two large buildings. For a moment Jessie stared at him unbelievingly. From her memories of Wild Bill Hickok, when she'd seen him on the stage in her younger days and when he'd visited the Circle Star, she was once again looking at Wild Bill in the flesh, as certain as she was that he was dead.

Jessie's surprise and her disbelief were not great enough to keep her from observing the newcomer closely as he walked toward her and Ramley. The man she saw was tall, wide-shouldered, and could have been any age from his middle thirties to his late forties. He had on the same long, black coat and wide-brimmed hat that she'd noted in her earlier glimpses of him in the semi-darkness at the de Mores chateau, and the overlong nose and full, drooping moustache were also just as she'd remembered.

Now, though, she was close enough to see his eyes, and they were brown instead of the ice-blue she recalled so clearly. His long hair, brushing the shoulders of his coat, was several shades lighter in hue than the color that had lodged in her memory from years past, and much coarser in texture.

Jessie took her eyes off the newcomer's face long enough to look at the ivory butts of the Colts belted on both hips. The revolvers Hickock had displayed with so much pride to her and Alex had been well-used, the ivory butts tinged with yellow, the hammers shining where the original blue finish had been worn away by long and frequent use. The Colts in the holsters worn by the man standing before her had the unmistakable look of weapons just out of the gunsmith's shop. Their butts were snow-white and the checkering on the hammers still as dark as when they'd come from the blueing bath.

"Who's the young lady?" he asked Ramley. "I'm sure I've seen her somewhere before."

"Not that it's any of your affair, but you've heard us talking about her enough," Ramley replied. "It's the Star-buck dame that's been giving us so much trouble at the frog's place."

"Of course. That's where I saw her." Turning to Jessie, he bowed deeply and said, "Miss Starbuck. I suppose you recognize me, even though there've been exaggerated reports of my untimely demise? The name is James Butler Hickok. I am also called Wild Bill."

Jessie's mind during the time since she'd been captured by Ramley had been devoted almost exclusively to trying to devise a way to escape. She was now facing a situation she hadn't really foreseen. She took her time replying to the man impersonating the famous outlaw.

"I suppose everyone's heard of Wild Bill Hickok," she compromised by saying when she answered him. "But everyone I know about has also heard that Mr. Hickok was killed right here in the Dakota Territory several years ago."

"As I said a moment ago, there have been reports—" he began.

Ramley cut him short, breaking in to say, "All right, I heard all I can stand, Barnhill. Go find Creed and Brense and Forest while I tie this dame up. Tell 'em we need to have a talk. And don't waste time looking for Sparrow. He yelled at me when we rode in, so he'll be here any minute now."

"I suppose I'm also invited to join your talk?" the fake Hickok asked.

"You're into this as deep as anybody," Ramley replied. "So I guess you better be there. Now, start moving. We'll set down in the big room to hash this thing over."

Jessie had been tucking names into her memory while Ramley was giving his orders. Now she knew how many —or how few—men were in the night-riders' gang, but there were other things as well that she knew she must find out in order to end the night raids on Medora and on the de Mores chateau. She realized also that she must devise a way to keep the gang holed up until Ki had time to follow her trail through the river canyon. She had no doubt at all that he would do so.

As the Hickok imposter started away, she asked Ramley,

"I gather from what you were saying that you have an employer somewhere who isn't satisfied with the progress you're making in frightening the marquis. Am I right?"

A startled expression passed over Ramley's face, but he regained his composure quickly. "What you think you know and what the real case is might not be the same thing. But it won't make a bit of never-mind as far as you're concerned. Now, come on. I wanta get you put away before the others get here."

By the time the shadow of his horse's head on the ground told Ki that the time had come to turn back and rejoin Jessie, he decided not to wait until he came to a wide spot on the trail. He rode as close as he dared to the sinuous canyon's rim and dismounted, then walked still farther toward it.

He felt the dry soil beginning to crumble underfoot, and took a quick step backward to more solid ground. Then he gazed along the winding canyon in both directions, but the sinuous curves in its almost vertical walls limited his view in both directions. Not satisfied, but knowing that the irregular contours would block the vista no matter where he stopped, he remounted and rode until he'd reached the spot where the trail along the river-canyon met the more heavily traveled path which they'd followed from the chateau, and he reined in, waiting for Jessie to rejoin him.

As the minutes passed and she still did not arrive, he grew both worried and thoughtful. He nudged his mount into motion and rode east along the canyon rim, expecting to see her around each bend of the sinuous trail. Even in the rare spots where the surface of the baked earth was relatively soft, he could see only an occasional hoofprint that he was sure had been left by Jessie's horse. He stopped twice to examine the softer patches of ground, but only

155

after he'd made the third stop was he sure that Jessie and someone on a horse with hoofprints strange to him were riding together.

Even with all his care, Ki passed the spot where Jessie and her captor had descended to the floor of the river's canyon, without noticing that they'd left the rimside trail. When he'd passed the second soft spot without seeing the now-familiar prints, he turned his horse and began back-tracking.

As Jessie had anticipated while hoping that she would be wrong, Ramley led her to the better preserved of the two large buildings remaining at the abandoned mining camp. He did not offer to help her dismount; he merely indicated the ground and jerked his head. Jessie had already decided that the best course for her to follow was to appear to be cooperating, while taking her time in carrying out any orders Ramley gave her.

She swung out of her saddle and stood beside the horse, making no move to join Ramley when he started for the door. He stopped, turned, and said, "Well, come along. You know damn well I'll drag you if you act up and start being smart."

Jessie walked up to him and he stood aside, motioning to the door. The interior of the building was as barren in-side as its exterior had promised. The downstairs area was one big room divided by open partitions, for the doorways had no doors, and the windows no sashes. She saw at a glance that the main floor was divided into three rooms, one on either side of a wide hall that extended to the center, where a stairway led to the second floor. A door beside the stairway led to the third room, which extended across the back of the building.

Saddle tack was strewn in one of the side rooms; two heaps of blankets in the other. There were chairs and at least two more rumpled sets of blankets in the big room at the end of the hall. When Jessie reached the stairway and hesitated, Ramley, behind her, stepped into the room containing the saddlery long enough to pick up a small coil of heavy mending twine. Then he motioned for Jessie to go up the stairs.

Jessie realized belatedly that her judgment had been flawed when she decided to cooperate and wait for a chance to break free. She also realized that the time had passed for her to change the acquiescent attitude she'd adopted. Keeping her face expressionless and saying nothing, she went up the creaking steps, Ramley following her closely.

Four doorways, all of them without doors, opened off the top of the landing. The room into which Ramley waved Jessie was barren of furniture, and dust lay thick on its floor.

"This'll do," he said, nodding. "Turn around."

"There's no need to tie me up," Jessie protested, keeping her voice even and stifling her anger. "If you and the others are going to be downstairs, I wouldn't have a chance of getting past all of you."

"You likely wouldn't," he agreed. "But just to save all of us a lot of trouble, hold still while I tie you up."

He tied Jessie's wrists behind her, pulling the rope tight enough to hurt her, but she made no protest. Then he motioned for her to sit down, and while she extended her feet he secured her ankles.

"Now," Ramley said as he stood up and looked at his knots. "You won't be worrying about getting away, and neither will I."

"What're you planning to do with me?"

"Looking at you right now, I got a few ideas about

that," Ramley leered. "But I don't want to start no trouble with the others. We still got our job to finish up, or we don't get the rest of the pay coming to us."

"Who's paying you?" Jessie asked.

"You know I ain't going to tell you that. Me and the boys don't even call no names when we're talking to each other." He gave a final glance at the ropes on Jessie's wrists and ankles and nodded with satisfaction. Then he turned and went down the creaking stairs, leaving her to wonder what was coming next.

Chapter 14

As Ki backtracked, he rode slowly along the trail that wound along the canyon wall, looking now for signs of the hoofprints left by Jessie's horse. He also watched the rim of the river canyon more carefully, knowing that Jessie would have no reason to turn back in the direction of the chateau. This time he found the tracks he'd missed earlier, the disturbed area away from the trail where Jessie had dismounted.

Studying the scuffed ground, Ki soon had a clear picture of what must have happened. There was a small area near the drop-off where Ramley's bootprints were the only marks, and a larger space away from the rim where Jessie's small boots had left their imprints. Beyond this, Ramley's bootprints first mingled with Jessie's on the barren, yellowish dirt, then were superimposed on them. Closer to the rim, then on the trail leading down into the river canyon, Jessie's bootprints were almost obliterated by those of

Ramley, while the hoofprints of the horse occasionally appeared superimposed on both.

As clearly as though he'd been watching, Ki could see the little procession in his mind's eye: Jessie picking her way carefully down the precipitous zigzagging trail to the canyon floor, Ramley behind her, leading the horse. Grasping the reins of his own horse, Ki led the animal down the treacherous winding incline.

Jessie did not have long to wait before the other outlaws arrived to join Ramley. Even though they chose one of the rooms at the foot of the stairs in which to hold their confab, the lack of doors and windows in the abandoned mine building allowed her to hear every word they spoke when the first babble of their arrival died away and they settled down to business.

"There's too many things happened on this job that the boss didn't count on," Ramley said. "And this Starbuck dame and the Chink that's with her is one of 'em."

"Who the hell is she, anyways?" a voice new to Jessie broke in. "All of a sudden she was there at the Frenchy's place, and there ain't much gone right since then."

"How would I know who she is, Sparrow?" Ramley demanded.

"Didn't the boss say anything about looking out for her?"

"Not one damn word," Ramley answered. "All I know is that since she got here de Mores ain't the easy mark the boss made him out to be when he sent us to handle this job."

A third man spoke, one whose voice Jessie did not recognize as having heard before. "I've heard about her and the chink," he said. "When I was with Bannon somebody wanted a few new guns on a job down in Texas that she

160

was mixed up in. As it turned out, I didn't go, but—well, I heard she got the boys that did go crisscrossed someways, and the job never did go right. Anyhow, that funny name, Starbuck, stuck in my mind."

"And that's all you know, Creed?" one of the others asked.

"That's all," Creed replied. "But it's more'n you know, Forest."

"I don't see what's got us stuck," Forest went on. "We got her, let's get rid of her. Once she's outta the way, we can go on and finish our job."

"Now, wait a minute!" a fresh voice broke in. "When I accepted this part, I wasn't told anything about shooting anyone, even killing them! All I agreed to do was to perform my imitation of Wild Bill Hickok when it was required. Gentlemen, I am an actor, not a gunfighter."

"You don't have to tell us again, Barnhill," Ramley said. "That's all you talked about to me and Sparrow on the train coming out here, and I guess by now Brense and Forest and Creed has heard enough of it, too."

"You better listen to what Ramley says, Barnhill," Sparrow broke in. "If you know what's good for you, you'll shut up and do whatever him and me tells you to, or you might travel back to Hinky Dink's place in a long pine box!"

In the silence that fell on the group downstairs following Sparrow's threat, Jessie's mind was working at top speed. It had been a long time since she'd heard the name of Hinky Dink. The first time was far in the past, on an occasion when Alex and Ki had gone to Chicago. After they returned and were talking about the problems they'd solved, Hinky Dink had been mentioned. When Jessie had asked about the odd name her father had explained the political power and underworld connections of the grafting,

161

crooked alderman who was the boss of Chicago's notorious
First Ward.

Now, for the first time, Jessie was beginning to get a
clear picture of the chain of events in which she and Ki had
quite unwittingly become involved. She'd barely had time
to put the first pieces of the puzzle together from the scattered clues of names and places and events when the men
downstairs began talking again. She gave up trying to piece
loose ends together and returned her attention to the conversation between the local outlaws and the man who'd
been sent from Chicago to help them.

Ramley was saying, "Sparrow, you lay off Barnhill.
You been riding him ever since that first time he done his
Wild Bill Hickok act, when he didn't scare off the redskins
that works at the beef plant the way the boss figured he
would."

"Scare, hell!" the man called Sparrow snorted. "That act
he put on wouldn't spook a baby!"

"Shut up, dammit!" Ramley ordered the other outlaw.
"He's doing the best he knows how to handle the part of
the job he's getting paid for. Now let's get down to it.
What we've got to do first is figure out how we're going to
handle the Starbuck dame. Maybe with her out of the way
the Frenchman won't be such a tough nut."

"There ain't but one thing to do with her," one of the
others volunteered. "Put a bullet into her and plant her
where nobody's likely to run across her again."

"Wait a minute, Brense!" Barnhill broke in. "You're
talking about cold-blooded murder! I've killed a few men
on the stage, but that's as far as I ever want to go. I won't
take part in killing somebody!"

"You'll do what me and Sparrow tells you to do!" Ramley said. His voice was as hard as well-tempered steel.
"And we're going to do the job we was sent here for."

162

Stillness settled over the room below following Ramley's words. Jessie realized that unless Ki had discovered her trail and was on his way she'd have to engineer her own escape. She began searching the room with her eyes, looking for something she could use as a tool to help her get rid of her bonds and perhaps as a weapon after she was free, but except for a thick film of dust its floor was totally bare. Then Ramley broke the silence that had settled in the room below after his threat. She stopped looking, and listened.

"Brense," Ramley said, "you or one of your friends oughta know where we can get our hands on some dynamite. Maybe in Medora?"

"Medora?" the man addressed asked. "Hell, they ain't got no dynamite in that little two-bit store there; it ain't nothing but a Indian trading post that the Frenchman put in to keep all them Sioux he's got working from wandering off."

"How about one of the mines?" Ramley asked.

"There's not all that many mines left close around," Brense answered. "I guess we can get a few sticks, but we'll have to travel for it. I get the idea you figure to blow up the Frenchman's beef plant?"

"It's the easiest and quickest way I can see to get rid of it," Ramley replied. "Me and Sparrow's blown enough safes in our time to know how to handle the stuff."

"I'd say Bowman's the closest place we'd be likely to find some," Brense went on thoughtfully. "But it'll take a while to get there and back."

"How much of a while?"

"Three, four days, pushing a good horse."

"Start first thing in the morning, then," Ramley ordered. "And get back as quick as you can. Now that's settled. If we can't put that de Mores fellow outta business one way, we'll do it another."

"You mean we're not going to ride to the de Mores place again until he gets back?" Barnhill asked.

"That's right."

"Then I'm going to take off this wig and moustache," the actor said. "They're very hot and uncomfortable."

"Slayman told you to wear 'em all the time," Ramley said.

"He's in Chicago." For the first time an edge of pugnacity sounded in the actor's voice. "Nobody but you men are going to see me." He was silent for a moment then added, "There! That's better!"

"Well, I guess it's all right," Ramley said. "But stay outta the way of that Starbuck dame till we get rid of her, and keep the rest of the outfit on, you hear me?"

"Don't worry, Ramley," Barnhill replied. "I'm being paid to act, and I'll wear the proper costume when I need to."

"See that you do," Ramley grunted. He went on, "Now, then. I guess the next thing is to take care of the woman. Me and Sparrow will get rid of her, if the rest of you're too queasy to take on the job."

"If we're going to do it, we might as well get some fun out of her first," Sparrow suggested.

"Oh, I wasn't about to miss that," Ramley said.

"Now hold on!" Brense broke in. "If I go to Bowman, I'm gonna miss all the fun!"

"It's too late for you to leave today," Ramley told the other outlaw. "Start at daylight tomorrow; we'll be having our fun with the woman tonight, before you leave."

"And if we don't finish her off," Sparrow put in, "you can have another go at what's left of her when you get back. You won't miss a thing, Brense."

164

"I don't want any part of this!" Barnhill protested. "I've never—"

"Shut up!" Ramley snapped. "The only reason Slayman hired you to come here with us is to act like you're Wild Bill Hickok's ghost and spook the Sioux so they'll quit working for de Mores."

Slayman was another name Jessie recognized. Nate Slayman was aptly named, for in addition to having close political ties to Hinky Dink's political ring he operated one of the biggest slaughterhouses in Chicago. Consequently, he was one of the largest cattle buyers at the Livestock Exchange auctions.

After Alex's untimely death, Slayman had tried to get Jessie to agree to selling him all the steers shipped east each year by the Circle Star. When she'd refused, telling him that she intended to honor her father's commitments to supply other slaughterhouses, Slayman had stormed angrily out of their conference, threatening to have Circle Star steers banned from the Livestock Exchange auctions. The Exchange Board had paid no more attention to his bluster than Jessie did, but she'd learned through other cattle shippers of Slayman's crooked activities.

In the room downstairs Ramley was talking again, and Jessie concentrated on listening.

"We won't ride tonight," the gang's boss was saying. "Or tomorrow night, either."

"You figure the woman can last that long?" Sparrow asked.

"Hell, there's only six of us," Ramley replied. "And all of us—"

"Five," Barnhill broke in. "I told you I won't have any part in this!"

"You better do what I say," Ramley shot back. "How're you figuring the boss is going to pay you the rest of what he said he would if you don't stick with us?"

"I'll do what Slayman hired me to—act like Wild Bill Hickok," the actor replied. "But that's as far as I'll go."

"Well, maybe you'll change your tune after me and you has a little private talk," Ramley said. "Which we'll do, soon as I finish getting everybody straight for right now."

"I don't intend to stay and listen to you," Barnhill snapped. "I'll go outside and walk around until the rest of you get through with your plans, but I don't want any part of them. And don't wait for me to come to supper. The sight of you and these other animals makes me sick."

A pistol shot interrupted him, and splintered wood crackled. For a long moment Jessie heard nothing from the room below, then Ramley spoke again.

"You set tight and keep quiet, Barnhill. Next time I won't be so careful to miss you," the gang's leader said ominously. "I'm plumb sick of listening to you bellyache."

"Ah, don't pay any mind to Barnhill," Sparrow broke in. "He ain't going to give us no trouble. Go on and tell us what you got figured out."

"All right," Ramley said. "Now here's what I figure. When Brense gets back, we'll wait till dark, and then we'll set two charges, one at de Mores's house and the other one at the beef factory. Brense, you be sure to get plenty of fuse. We'll set a long fuse at the house and be in Medora before it goes off. We'll short-fuse the beef factory so when it blows up de Mores will be too busy to leave that fancy house he's got. And that oughta just about wind him up, as far as the beef factory's concerned. All we'll have to do is go back and get the rest of our pay from Slayman."

"Sounds good to me," Sparrow said.

"Sure does," Creed agreed. "It oughta work out fine. Hell, when me and Brense and Forest get our pay, we won't have to pull no more jobs for a long time."

"What I want to know is when we start on the woman," Forest said. "Since you told us we'd all get a whack at her, I been getting a mite anxious to plow in. She's a damn fine looker."

"Soon as we finish supper," Ramley promised. "I don't know about the rest of you, but my belly's telling me it's been a long time since we had that little bite after we got back. I ain't real sure whether I'm hornier or hungrier. Anyways, I aim to eat before I do anything else. Let's go over to the old cookshack and fire up the stove."

"What about the woman?" Sparrow asked.

"She'll be all right where she's at. Maybe if she's hungry enough she'll be a little bit easier to handle when we get back."

Jessie heard the thunking of their boots on the board floor below her as the outlaws left the building. Then all was quiet.

Ki reached the bottom of the canyon and found that he now had a well-marked trail to follow along the riverbank. The prints of the horse ridden by Jessie were by now as familiar to him as the lines on his own palm. To a tracker of Ki's skill and experience, the story told by the prints he'd seen on the canyon rim and along its floor told an almost complete story: Jessie had been taken by surprise by a man who had been lurking behind the outlaw gang.

Knowing Jessie, he was surprised that she'd been captured without a struggle, but the evidence was plain that she had. It was also clear to Ki that the man who'd surprised her was also forcing her to go with him—obviously to a hideout farther along the riverbank.

Forewarned, Ki took no chances. He followed the hoofprints swiftly, but not recklessly. When he saw the clustered buildings of the abandoned mine looming ahead, he

167

reined in. Tethering his horse, he started toward the buildings on foot, using the scant vegetation to screen his *ninja* moves.

When he drew close enough to the dilapidated buildings to hear the men talking inside one of them, Ki exercised double caution. He was still too far away to make out their words, but even at a distance the varying timbres of their voices enabled him to count the number of speakers. He strained his ears, trying to hear Jessie's voice, and finally decided that she was being held somewhere else while the outlaws talked.

His concentration on the babble of the outlaws talking inside did not take Ki's attention away from his stealthy approach. He used the derelict buildings and the debris that strewed the ground around them for cover, and was within a dozen yards of his objective when Ramley's pistol shot cracked through the canyon's still air.

For a moment, Ki stopped and flattened himself motionless on the ground. When no outcries or agitated voices broke the quiet, he moved again. This time he did not use the time-consuming invisible *ninja* approach, but flattened himself on the ground and crawled as fast as he dared move until he reached its wall. Then he became a *ninja* again, a shadow rippling on the barren soil, circling the base of the big barnlike structure until he was below one of the windows of the room from which the voices came.

Ramley was speaking, giving orders to Brense, when Ki came to a halt below the window. Ki listened in vain for Jessie's voice, and began to worry when he did not hear it. Ramley's reference to her a moment later eased his mind, and though he'd found the talk about dynamite more than a bit unpleasant, he realized that when the outlaws deferred their next move against de Mores, that left him only Jessie to think about in the immediate future.

Waiting until the gang trooped out for supper, Ki levered himself through the yawning window opening and began to search for Jessie. After quick glances into the downstairs rooms of the deserted building he went upstairs and found her.

"I've been expecting you, Ki," Jessie said calmly when he reached the room upstairs where she lay bound on the floor. "I didn't know when to expect you, but I knew you'd turn up sooner or later."

As he worked at the knots in the rope that was immobilizing Jessie, Ki said, "I'd have been here sooner, but I waited until those outlaws cleared out downstairs. I could've gotten past them easily enough, but I wanted to hear as much as I could about what they're planning to do next."

"You heard the same thing I did, then," she replied. As she spoke, Jessie was rubbing the weals left by the rope that had bitten into her arms. She went on, "I suppose it's too soon for you to have any ideas about the best way to handle them?"

"A little bit soon, but we've got plenty of time. They're not planning to move until the one who's going after the dynamite gets back. What about the man who's been posing as Wild Bill Hickok's ghost?" he went on, frowning thoughtfully. "From what I overheard, he's certainly not in favor with the others anymore."

"He's just an actor, Ki. I don't know how dependable he'd be if he wasn't just playing a part."

"I'll be just as dependable as I can," Barnhill's voice came from the doorway.

Jessie and Ki looked around in unison, and their jaws dropped. Without his Wild Bill Hickok makeup, the actor looked like the old man he was. The flowing moustache and wig had taken years from his appearance; his face was

169

seamed with a maze of wrinkles, and his lips were broken by tiny vertical lines. He'd discarded the wide-brimmed hat with the long wig Jessie had seen him in before, and except for a fringe of short white hair above his ears he was totally bald.

"You certainly wouldn't've fooled anybody without your make-up," Jessie said.

"I wouldn't have tried," he agreed. "You're right, of course. I am just an actor, but I came up here to untie you and offer to help you. If you think I can, count on me to do anything you ask."

Jessie and Ki had recovered from their surprise by the time Barnhill finished speaking. They exchanged glances, and, in the silent communication which they'd come to share after so many years of common danger, reached agreement instantly.

"Your help will be very welcome," Jessie said.

"I guess you heard enough when we were talking downstairs to know how I got involved with these outlaws in the first place," Barnhill went on.

"I did," Jessie replied. She turned to Ki and asked, "Had you gotten here when Mr. Barnhill and that one called Ramley had their disagreement?"

Ki shook his head. "The first thing I heard when I got close enough was Ramley sending one of the others to find some dynamite. I guessed that since their attacks on the chateau weren't successful, they planned to blow it up."

"There's quite a lot more to it than that," Jessie told him. "Much too long to tell now. But it all goes back to Chicago. You remember Nate Slayman, I'm sure."

"I remember him well; you and Alex both had some problems with him," Ki replied. "And everything I can think of about him is bad. But how does he figure in this, Jessie? The Dakota Territory is a long way from Chicago."

"Oh, Slayman's not here himself," Jessie explained. "But he's the one who sent Mr. Barnhill and the others out here. He must be losing a great deal of business to the marquis's beef factory, so he sent Brense and the other two Chicago thugs—and Mr. Barnhill, of course, to—" Jessie stopped short and shook her head. "It's a long story, Ki, too long to go into now. We'd better be out of this place before those thugs get back. I'll finish telling you later."

Chapter 15

Jessie, Ki, and Barnhill had barely reached the foot of the stairs when the voices of the outlaws sounded outside, signaling their return. Though the approaching men were not yet near enough for their words to be understood, the fugitives knew they must move fast.

"In here," Jessie said, leading them into one of the small rooms in the front part of the abandoned building. "When they start talking, we can crawl out one of the window openings. If we're lucky we'll have time to get away before they discover I'm not upstairs."

Ki and Barnhill followed her into the bare room. They hugged the wall beside the bare hole that had been a doorway just as the footsteps of the renegades thudded on the steps.

"We'll keep it simple, and handle it fair," Ramley was saying to his men as they followed him inside. "One hand of straight five-card stud, all the cards dealt face-up. High man gets first crack at the Starbuck dame; low man's last."

"That ain't as fair as it sounds," Brense complained. "I got to do a lot of riding to get that dynamite, and you promised me I'd have a go at her before I left."

"So I did," Ramley agreed. "And I'll keep my word, Brense. You deal, and set out of the game, then. High hand goes next after you've had your fun."

Pressed to the wall in the room just off the entrance, Jessie listened to the voices of the plug-uglies. She shuddered in spite of herself when she heard their words, and thought of the gang rape she'd so narrowly escaped. However, her moment of relief was brief and the needs of the immediate future urgent. She waited for the outlaws to go through the wide entrance hall, and when their voices faded as the last of them left the entry, she motioned for Ki and Barnhill to lean closer.

"We'll wait until they start playing that showdown hand they were talking about," she whispered. "If we give them time to deal two or three cards, they'll be so interested in their gambling that they won't even hear us slip out the window."

"There are plenty of hiding places we can duck into," Ki suggested. Not quite sure how quickly their new companion could react either physically or mentally, he added, "Barnhill, you know the layout here better than either Jessie or I do. You go first. Pick out an empty building and head for it. Don't bother stopping to look back; Jessie and I will be right behind you."

By now the conversation from the big room where the outlaws had gone was more subdued. Then one of the men said loudly enough to override the others, "Dammit, Brense, you don't need to shuffle that deck again! Lay it down so one of us can cut it and start dealing!"

"Just hold your horses," Brense told him. "I wouldn't

want anybody to think I didn't do a good job of shuffling."

In the silence that fell after the exchange, they could hear the faint clicking of the cards being shuffled. There was a long moment of silence. Then Brense said, "If you pair up on either one of them picture cards you got, you're going to be next after me with the woman, Forest."

"Quit jabbering, dammit!" one of the others snapped. "Just deal the cards!"

"Now!" Jessie whispered to Barnhill. "We'll have to go out the window; they'll see us if we try to get to the door. Move fast, but don't make any noise!"

Showing surprising agility, the old actor straddled the windowsill, swung his feet out, and levered himself off his perch. Even Jessie and Ki barely heard the soft thud of his feet as he hit the ground. They lost no time in following him, and stood for a moment looking around, seeking a place that would conceal them.

There was a surprisingly large choice. Some of the long-departed miners who'd established the camp had apparently tried their luck at placer mining, for here and there along the riverbank there were big heaps of sand that could only have come from the bottom of the shallow stream. In the other direction, between them and the canyon wall, beyond the building where the outlaws were gambling for Jessie there were a dozen or more ramshackle shanties and two more good-sized buildings.

"There are only two things we can do," Jessie said as they huddled beside the wall. "Either get out of the canyon now or wait until dark, when we might have a better chance."

"Let's get out now, if we can," Ki suggested. "So far we've found places to hide when we needed them, but the odds here in the canyon are two to one against us."

Jessie nodded. "I feel the same way."

Barnhill broke in to say, "Whatever you decide is all right with me. I get the idea that you've had a lot more experience at this sort of thing than I have."

"Where do they deep the horses?" Ki asked him. "We'll need them if we're going to get away."

"There's a corral down past the houses," he replied. "We had to fix it up a little bit, but that's where they keep them."

"Then that's the place we'd better head for," Jessie said. "Where's your horse, Ki?"

"I left it at the foot of the trail leading out of the canyon. I couldn't be sure whether or not you were here."

"Mine's probably in the corral with the others," she went on. "And Mr. Barnhill's is sure to be there. You can ride double with me from the corral to the trail out."

They started inching along the side of the building and had almost reached its corner when a yell sounded inside and booted feet began pounding the floor.

"What's wrong, Ramley?" they heard one of the outlaws call.

"She's gone!" Ramley shouted. "Slipped the damn ropes and I guess jumped out the window! Scatter out, fast! Maybe she's holed up in one of the shacks, but somebody better get the hell down to the corral, too! If we hurry we'll find her before she's had time to get outta the canyon!"

Feet thudded again as the outlaws ran from the building. Jessie, Ki, and Barnhill pressed against the building wall. They heard the outlaws calling as they scattered, and as the cries faded they edged to the corner of the wall and peered around it.

Two or three men were visible, their backs turned, as they moved between the ramshackle buildings, peering through glassless windows and the yawning gaps of doors.

176

At a little distance they heard the men who'd headed for the corrals or who were searching around the tall heaps of dirt which were scattered between the riverbank and the canyon walls.

"It seems to me the safest place for us to be is right here where we are," Ki observed. "They'll be straggling back in a little while, when they don't find you."

"Yes," Jessie agreed. "They might even think I've already left the canyon and started up the trail."

"I've noticed that they're all going downstream," Barnhill said thoughtfully. "Wouldn't the safe thing for us to do be to go the other way?"

"It might be, except for one thing," Ki replied. "There might be no trail out of the canyon in that direction. We'd be trapped."

"I can see that," Barnhill agreed. "And if they were to catch up with us and it came to a fight, we wouldn't have much chance against double our number."

"I'm not sure we'll be able to get out without fighting," Jessie said. "Which reminds me. Would you object to letting me use one of your pistols?"

"Certainly not! And I see that Ki isn't armed; he can use the other one if he wants it," Barnhill offered. "To tell you the truth, the only times I've fired a gun of any kind before coming here were on the stage, just shooting a powder charge."

"Ki has his own weapons," Jessie explained. "Keep the second gun yourself. It's quite likely that you'll need it." As an afterthought she asked, "It is loaded, I hope?"

"Yes, indeed. Ramley insisted that I keep a bullet in every hole in the—the cylinder," Barnhill said. "And I have more in my pocket. The part I was playing required me to know how to load and unload the weapon, so I do know how to do that much."

While Jessie was inspecting the heavy ivory-grip Colt .44 that Barnhill handed her, Ki edged even closer to the corner of the wall and peered around it.

"I don't see any of them right now," he said. "But they're going to be coming back soon, after they fail to find us."

"And they've already searched the area around here." Jessie nodded. "Yes, it's not likely there'll be a better time until after dark, so let's move now. If we see any of them coming, we can duck into one of the cabins."

Searching their surroundings with watchful eyes, they left the cover of the building and started for the higgledy-piggledy group of shanties. They reached it without hearing an alarm raised, and they dodged between the falling, decrepit little shacks until they reached the last one.

Ki peered around the edge of the tumbledown shanty, then turned back to Jessie and Barnhill. He said, "There aren't any more cabins ahead, just clumps of grass between here and a rope corral where they keep the horses."

"We don't have much choice," Jessie pointed out. "We've got to have horses if we expect to get away."

"And the outlaws know that," Ki replied. "They're probably heading for the same place we are. We'd better go one by one. The three of us together make too much of a target."

"That'll be better, yes," Jessie agreed.

"Then if it's all right with you, Jessie, I'll go first," he went on.

"Go ahead," she said. "Mr. Barnhill can go next, and the two of you can cover me when you get to the next shelter."

Bending low, Ki started running across the arid, clumped ground. He was within a few steps of the corral when a shout sounded from the area between them

178

and the trail to the canyon's rim. A shot followed the shout. The bullet kicked up dust between Ki and the corral. Jessie glanced toward the spot where the shout had come from. She saw a moving man and fired, but he kept running toward a pile of dirt and vanished behind it.

"Run!" she told Barnhill. "Go join Ki!"

Bending as he'd seen Ki do, the actor ran. He'd almost reached his goal when a revolver cracked and he staggered. He stayed on his feet and continued running until he was within a yard or two of the grass clump where Ki had taken cover, then lurched forward and fell sprawling.

Jessie broke cover now. She saw a man running toward them, and she snapped off a quick shot at him. He raised his revolver, but Jessie's shot reached him before he could take aim. He fell, spinning with the impact of the heavy slug from the Colt.

Ki was already hurrying to Barnhill's side. Just as another shot rang out and lead sang over his head, he grabbed the fallen man by the armpits and dragged him into the sparse shelter of the waving grasses. The next hunk of lead that spit from the rifleman's gun sailed over the heads of Ki and Barnhill just as Jessie dived into the grass to join them.

Shouts were sounding beyond the area where the man with the rifle had stationed himself. Ki was bending over Barnhill now. The old actor was still conscious, clinging to his senses by sheer force of will.

Through gritted teeth, his words garbled and throaty, he said "Funny—it doesn't—hurt—inside. But—I feel like —a mule just—kicked me—in my stomach."

Ki's eyes flicked over the wounded man's prone form and saw the blood spreading over his trousers below his hips.

"It probably hit a muscle," he assured the wounded

179

man. "Hang on. Jessie and I will tend to you as soon as we can."

Two bullets, one on either side of the grass clump, kicked up small bursts of earth as they narrowly missed their target. Jessie looked at Barnhill's recumbent form and saw there was nothing she could do to help him. Then she peered through the screening brush, her borrowed Colt poised and ready.

Another shot, this one from close by, thudded into the soil and raised a puff of dust at its edge. Jessie saw a sliver of movement in a small clump of brush thirty yards from their improvised fortress. She had her Colt ready when the man who'd sheltered there rose to fire again. Her revolver roared and the man pitched forward, his gun dropping from his lifeless hand.

"If you can cover our new friend, I'll make a *ninja* crawl on them and see if I can relieve our situation," Ki told her.

Absorbed in studying the terrain, Jessie nodded. Ki dropped to the ground, and when Jessie took her eyes off the terrain where the outlaws were assembling to glance at him again, he'd vanished. She went back to watching the barren terrain and the heaps of dirt that rose above its scanty knee-high growth of yellowing long-stem prairie grass and an occasional stunted juniper bush.

Jessie's patient watchfulness was rewarded sooner than she'd expected. The man in the brush-clump rose to his knees, his head and shoulders above the thin growth that had hidden him. Jessie raised the Colt, but before she could sight for a shot a silver arc flashed through the air and the outlaw clutched his throat for a moment before pitching forward and lying still.

From a spot to one side of the fallen man another of the outlaws stood up, and only seconds were needed for Jessie to swing the Colt to cover him and trigger off her shot. The heavy slug sent the renegade toppling backward as his gunhand sagged. He crumpled to the ground and lay as still as was the form of the one who'd been Ki's target.

A hundred yards down the canyon floor, another of the outlaws broke cover. He began running toward his fallen fellows, zigzagging as he moved. Jessie tried to follow him in the Colt's sights, but his movements were timed with an experience which she recognized as having been gained in many such affrays. She still kept her Colt ready, but knowing that she had at most three and possibly only two more cartridges she held her fire, waiting until he was near enough for a certain shot.

Before he'd covered half the distance that Jessie was waiting for him to close, she saw the arching flash of another of Ki's *shuriken*. The second blade sailed as true as had the first. The outlaw was in mid-stride when it sank into his throat, but he finished the stride he'd been making and half of another before he began to droop. Then death caught up with his momentum and, like the first of Ki's targets, he lurched and fell forward and sprawled in a motionless heap.

A pistol barked at one side of Jessie's position, and she dropped prone at once. The slug would have fallen short even if it had been well-aimed. She saw the spurt that the whistling bullet raised when it plowed into the canyon floor ten feet to one side of where she lay.

Moving very carefully, Jessie began to get to her knees. She was raising her head to scan the valley floor again when a sighing groan behind her reached her ears. Still on her knees, she turned to see Barnhill standing at her side, his torso swaying, his face contorted with pain. Both his hands were closed around the butt of the Colt she'd insisted

181

he keep, and he was lifting the weapon slowly, his eyes fixed on some spot beyond her.

Jessie was turning to look over her shoulder when the pistol in Barnhill's hands barked and a spurt of flame jetted from its muzzle. Behind her another shot rang out and she completed her half-turn in time to see Sparrow crumpling to the ground only a few yards behind her, the pistol he'd been aiming dropping from his hands.

Jessie jumped to her feet and stepped to Barnhill's side. His body was beginning to sag, and blood was seeping out of a fresh wound in his shoulder. She grasped his upper arms to steady him, and as he slumped to the ground she held on to help him drop gently instead of plunging down.

"I'll help you down," she said. "It looks like you've just got a flesh wound."

"It felt like I stepped in front of a locomotive," the old actor gasped as she helped him stretch out on the ground. "But the funny thing is, I don't hurt where the bullet went in."

Jessie looked at the small trickle of blood seeping from his shoulder, and was about to turn away when another patch of blood on his clothing caught her eye. Red was glistening on Barnhill's trousers, and as Jessie looked at it she saw that it was increasing in slow spurts.

She looked for the wound that had set off the flow and saw the small black hole just below his belt on his right side. Her heart sank. She'd seen similar bullet-wounds during the days of battle she and Ki had gone through in their long struggle against the cartel. She knew the bullet had torn through Barnhill's femoral artery, which was buried so deeply inside his body that it could be reached only by a surgeon's scalpel.

"Just keep as still as you can," she told Barnhill. "I'll see what I can do for you."

182

"All of us actors learn to read voices, Miss Starbuck," he said, grasping Jessie's wrist. "Yours says I'm going to die. Am I right?"

"I'll try to—"

Barnhill broke in before Jessie could finish the promise that she was trying to make to ease his mind. He shook his head gently as he told her, "Dying doesn't frighten me, dear lady. I've outlived my time, or I wouldn't't've come out here to portray Wild Bill Hickok's ghost. And I did a good job, played the role well, don't you think?"

"It was an excellent performance," she assured him. "You had all of us half-believing that Wild Bill had really come back to life."

"Ahh," he sighed. "Thank you, my dear Miss Starbuck. Applause is the sweetest music ever to reach an actor's—"

Barnhill's voice lost its resonance and faded to silence as his arms went limp and his head rolled to one side. His Wild Bill Hickok hat had fallen beside his shoulder. She reached for it and was covering Barnhill's face with its broad, flat rim when a shot broke the stillness and a slug kicked up a spurt of dust from the sandy soil only inches away from her.

Jessie dropped flat and reached for the Colt that had fallen from the dead actor's hand. No second shot sounded, and she raised her head carefully to look for the outlaw who'd fired. She saw his outline silhouetted against the bright sky. He was crouching in a clump of scant prairie grass a dozen yards away.

When Jessie saw that the crouching man was Ramley she raised the Colt in her hand. Before either she or the outlaw could aim and fire the glint of flying steel flashed across the blue sky in a shining arc and Ki's *shuriken* bit into Ramley's throat.

His gunhand sagging, Ramley's dying reflex triggered

the shot he'd been about to loose at Jessie. The heavy slug raised dust only a few yards away from him as Ramley lurched forward, off balance, his final gesture a vain effort to reach the blade that had severed his carotid artery and was draining his life's blood in pulsing gouts.

Beyond the outlaw's body Ki abandoned his flattened half-invisible *ninja* position and stood up.

"Are you all right, Jessie?" he called.

"Yes. But be careful, Ki. There may be some of the other outlaws within range."

"No. Ramley was the last one. I've been keeping track of them," he replied as he started walking toward her. He saw Barnhill's body then and asked as he came to stand beside Jessie, "Was it Ramley who shot him, Jessie?"

She nodded. "Yes. But not until Barnhill had saved my life with a shot that would have done credit to Wild Bill Hickok himself. He may have gotten out of character now and then, Ki, but he played his role until the very end. And maybe that's the way he'd have wanted to die. Now, suppose we go back to the chateau and tell the marquis what's happened. Then we'll get on the next train and go home to the Circle Star."

Watch for

LONE STAR AND THE DEADLY STRANGER

seventy-first novel in the exciting
LONE STAR
series from Jove

coming in July!